"Confess, you are not the Contessa D'Alessandria."

Sir Maxim's bright blue eyes pierced Kate's very soul.

"*Certamente*, I am the Contessa. You insult me with this mirthless joke of yours." Kate snapped open her fan and waved it energetically before her.

"I can prove quite easily that you are not who you say you are," said Sir Maxim as he moved closer to her and put a hand on her waist. "The real Contessa has a mole, and I know where it is to be found."

Kate thrust her fan up between their faces. "You know where it is and I know where it is and that is enough. No man treats the Contessa D'Alessandria like a strumpet." With a decided snap that sounded very much like a slap, she shut her fan. "I had thought better of you, sir. How sad to be so disappointed."

As she left him in the moonlight, Sir Maxim decided that *he* was not at all disappointed—he was intrigued!

Books by Coral Hoyle

HARLEQUIN REGENCY ROMANCE
4–MIDSUMMER MASQUE
15–THE VIRGIN'S HEART

A MERRY GO-AROUND

CORAL HOYLE

Harlequin Books

TORONTO • NEW YORK • LONDON
AMSTERDAM • PARIS • SYDNEY • HAMBURG
STOCKHOLM • ATHENS • TOKYO • MILAN

To all the scoundrels
I've known and loved,
and
to Marmie
for her kindheartedness

Published July 1990

ISBN 0-373-31129-X

PROLOGUE

"IT'S ALL VERY WELL to say she's supposed to be one, but, try as she might, Kate just doesn't have the look of a paramour." To better survey his sister, Anthony McClintock lit a few more candles in their private parlour of the White Hart Inn.

Kate slowly turned, allowing her two brothers to appreciate fully her newly-acquired maid's labours. She cast them a saucy grin. "Do remember that I am the Contessa D'Alessandria. Since being widowed at a very young age, I've become a woman of great renown."

Her younger brother, Polonius, walked around her shaking his head. "There's something missing. You have her pleasing shape, so we won't need any upper padding...but there's something not quite right." He looked at her through narrowed eyes. "I have it! Your attitude is all wrong. You have no style. That's the trouble with an untried soubrette." He struck a pose. "Your shoulders must come back...as if you want your charms admired. And throw your head back...like so...as if you want a man to take you in his arms. Then place your hand high on your hip...and purse your lips. Ah! There, you have it! What do you think, Tony?"

Known to have a keen eye for detail, Anthony scanned his sister from head to toe beginning with her creamy skin, tinged with a healthy hint of colour at her cheeks. Below her delicate nose, the fullness of her lower lip was disciplined by the perfect bow of its counterpart. For her role of coquette, her rich brown hair had been artfully arranged in a stylish manner. Yet a directness of gaze from her green eyes gave her that stamp of quality not found in a woman of lesser breeding. Her regal carriage gave distinction to her above average inches. Though a daughter of a thespian, she had the appearance of an aristocrat—something which had always eluded the real Contessa.

"There's no way to hide it," Anthony remarked. "Kate has the look of a virgin."

The tone of disappointment in her older brother's voice and the sigh of resignation from her younger brother were too much for Kate. She burst out laughing. "Don't be too downcast, my dears. Perhaps, with a bit of luck, I'll manage to ruin myself."

Polonius glared at her. "A good actor—even an amateur like yourself—can play a part without first having to live it. Maybe a cosmetic application would serve."

Kate grimaced. "Spare me, please. As I remember when we were children, you always made me look dead. I'd rather wear a heavy veil."

"Aha! Just the thing we need." Anthony strode from the room. Shortly he returned with a large black square of finely woven netting. Draping it over her head, he stood back to see the effect. "Perfect! Even someone acquainted with the Contessa would be fooled."

"If you can remember to stand and move in the same manner as the Contessa," Polonius said, trying to see through the veil, "you'll make a first-rate impostor."

"But only if you master a little Italian, first, *cara signora*," warned her elder brother. Having recently sold out, Lieutenant Anthony McClintock had learned a few Italian phrases while serving on the Island of Malta, and so had been given the task of tutoring her. "Papa will not be pleased if you do not capture the essence of the Contessa's speech . . . that slight accent in a low, husky whisper."

Kate plucked the veil from her head and glared at her brothers. "I didn't ask to be a Contessa. I was quite satisfied residing in Leicester, letting old Mrs. Bagworth beat me at cards."

"Ha!" scoffed Polonius, "what a bouncer. You were languishing from boredom. You required rescuing. Dashed dull being a lady's companion. Besides, when have you ever said nay to Papa when he needed you? Demme, Kate, you're the most amiable girl I know . . . and I know a great many females."

"It's all very well to be agreeable," she said, "but it's devilish hard to be so in a disagreeable situation. However is Papa to succeed in this charade?"

"The only thing he knows better than a stage is cards. He's a gamester," Anthony said matter-of-factly, "so he'll have weighed the odds. He'll take the trick. He must carry it off. For there's fifteen thousand guineas at stake! Even now, Papa's in the tap-room getting the lay of the land."

Not far from them, on the opposite side of the inn, their father stood at the bar downing a bit of ale. His listeners waited patiently as Henry McClintock quenched his thirst. Fabrication was dry work, and Henry had been labouring with a vigour born of a fecund mind.

"Aye, lads," Henry said, setting his tankard down, "it was a glorious sight. His Majesty looked like his old self as he sat there listening to the lovely Contessa sing. She'd captured his heart as she'd done with so many before. All the great ones demand to hear her. Even that heathen, Bonaparte, ordered her brought to him when she'd been taken prisoner as she tried to flee." Henry slapped his palm to the bar. "But she would not sing for him. Not even after he put her in the Bastille. She is as brave as she is beautiful."

"And she's stayin' right here in the White Hart," the innkeeper said proudly.

"Seems queer that a lady who knows the King should be stayin' here," an anonymous traveller stated. "Why ain't this Contessa in London with all the lords and ladies?"

"Ah, my good fellow," Henry said jovially, "the dear Contessa wished to go among the simple people of England and see for herself the beauties of our land. She had too many admirers in Town. A duel was being fought every day just to determine who would have the honour of driving her through the Park. The lady longed for peace and quiet."

"Well, she'll not get it at a coaching inn," observed the weary traveller.

The innkeeper blustered. "The White Hart is a superior establishment, sir. Not only is it frequented by the wayfarer, but many of our local gentry come here to enjoy the ale—the best in Bedfordshire—and the genial company. Squire Colley keeps a table regular-like just over there by the fire. I expect he'll be coming in at his usual time this evening."

"To the White Hart!" Henry said, raising his tankard in salute, "and the good folk of Biggleswade."

"To beautiful women," a young buck said, as he teetered on his feet.

"I drink to the Contessa D'Alessandria," Henry said, his voice touched with a reverence that caught at the heart of his fellows.

"To the King," another said. Soon the tankards were clanging together in a continual chorus of toasts that went on until the taproom seemed to ring from the revelry.

But with work still to be done, Henry McClintock cornered the innkeeper and drew him aside for a quiet word or two.

"My good man," Henry said, "tell me more about your townsfolk, especially Squire Colley."

The boastful innkeeper regaled his listener with all the histories of the gentry within a ten-mile radius of Biggleswade. Saving the best for the last, he told of Squire Colley. "Though some say he's bird-witted—from humble origins, you understand—there's those who hold to it that the Squire's a bell-swagger. Always clanging about calling attention to his own importance, being the magistrate and all. Squire Jethro Gillingham Colley!''

"A leader in the community, is he?"

"Aye, Squire's father left his only child well-off. There was coal under the gaffer's fingernails, but his son's hands were never soiled.'' The man behind the bar looked down at his own work-roughened hands and spat over his shoulder. "Squire lives in Ivel Manor now. The gaffer bought the land about the place and turned it into a large, fine piece of property. These five years or more, the Squire's reigned at the manor with his mother.''

"The Squire is a bachelor, then?"

"Aye! And he does like the wenches. Many's the time, though, he's told me that he's not maggot-brained enough to settle on one woman unless she's got a handsome portion coming with her. Now, some would say he has his eye on his cousin's widow, who's been stayin' with 'em up there at the manor. But some think the recent arrival of that lady's own brother, Sir Maxim Wolverton, bodes ill for the Squire's plans.''

"Wolverton? The name has a sound of importance. One of our older families, perhaps?"

"It's said he's well-connected with many of the titled families.'' The innkeeper leaned closer, pretending to wipe a particular spot on the bar. "Word's about that Sir Maxim's come to challenge the Squire. A dishonoured lady must be avenged, so they say.''

Henry feigned a look of shock. "Then I must protect the dear Contessa from such a rogue.''

"If Squire takes a fancy to her she'll find a wealthy protector in him.'' The innkeeper leered and winked at Henry. "He thinks hisself lucky with the ladies and the cards—a regular buck of the first order."

"Ah! Then the Squire is a gaming man?" At the fellow's nod of assent, Henry smiled. "Perhaps—just perhaps, mind you—a meeting *might* be arranged," Henry said pausing in happy contemplation, "so that I may determine if the gentleman would make a fit acquaintance for the Contessa. One cannot be too careful these days. Landlord, you must make me known to this gentleman and others of his ilk." His eyes twinkled as he began silently to reckon the pickings he would take from the good folk of Biggleswade.

CHAPTER ONE

ON THE FRONT OF THE PORTICO of Ivel Manor the initials *JGC* blazed, announcing the ownership of the fine estate to those who passed by. In the Grand Salon, a gilded *JGC* was prominent in the plasterwork on the ceiling and it was chiselled in the marble of the fireplace. It was woven in the pattern of the draperies and chairs. The initials could be found upon anything and everything of cost or importance to the Squire.

Sitting at her ease in her guise as the Contessa, Kate surveyed all that was Jethro Gillingham Colley's. She deduced from her observations that no one thought more of himself than the Squire. Concealed behind the black half veil, which was fastened to the protruding brim of her cottage bonnet, she could watch her host and his mother without appearing rude. They were an amusing pair.

Mrs. Penelope Colley, clearly an eccentric, wore a morning dress known as the polonaise, which had been fashionable in a previous era. Yet, oddly, she was appropriately gowned. For the oval hoop and full overskirt were required to disguise her very wide hips. A pink powdered Pompadour wig of shocking height drew the eye upward to the fanciful beribboned cap atop her curls.

Her inclinations seemed to favour the French Royalists, as exemplified by the ornate furnishings in the room, which were from the Louis periods. Surrounded by her son's numerous and grandiose possessions, Mrs. Colley looked at home in their recreated age of elegance.

The Squire, on the other hand, had the appearance of a man snatched out of a hunting print. His riding dress, though inappropriate for receiving guests, set off his manly attributes. His proud stance suggested a chest full of air. He'd struck a pose by the salon fireplace when Kate and her father had arrived and, as yet, he'd not wavered from his posturing.

"It is my opinion," The Squire intoned, "that a common coaching inn is hardly the place for a lady of the Contessa's rank and beauty. I make no doubt that she's plagued day *and* night by unseemly fellows." He drew breath, swelling his chest further. "For her own good I insist she accept my protection." At his mother's gasp he amended, "That is, the protection of my house . . . and the watchful care of m' mother."

"Your *sentiments* do you credit, Squire," Henry said, casting his daughter a sidelong glance. "But we could not take advantage of such a generous offer. You must understand that the Contessa travels not only with myself, but with her maestro, her bodyguard and her abigail. No, no, I must refuse you . . . even though I know that the Contessa would be most comfortable in this regal house."

Kate beckoned to her father. He hurried to her side and bowed. They conferred briefly in low voices.

"I thought your purpose was to gain an invitation," she whispered.

"My dear," he murmured, "one should not appear too eager, lest the pigeon take flight. Leave this to your Papa." Henry stepped away to converse with the Squire. Leading the younger man along, he began to take the fellow into his confidence. "What I am about to tell you must go no further. I can see that you are a man of discretion. Your repute is known throughout the county." He refrained from saying that his host had a reputation as a great gossip.

The Squire appeared eager at first, then his eagerness turned to uneasiness. "I mustn't keep secrets from m' mother. She doesn't like that." He glanced over at her. "She may look the eccentric, but, as she often says, all truly great ladies are considered unusual. It's quite the fashionable thing. But under that wig, she's a clever one."

"Ah! No doubt she has a fine perception that must be consulted. Come." Henry took the Squire's arm.

The two men joined Mrs. Colley. They each drew up a chair by the striped sofa where she sat, fully occupying its entire breadth with an overflow of skirt. Henry adjured them to lean nearer so that the Contessa would not hear.

"I am about to tell you of a great tragedy," Henry said, his voice heavy with sadness. "You may have remarked upon the Contessa's black veil and gloves. She honours the, ah, mourning rituals of her homeland, for she grieves over the loss of a *very* dear friend." In an aside to the Squire, he muttered, "A close, particular friend . . . if you take my meaning."

Fretfully, Mrs. Colley plucked at the neckerchief that lay insipidly across her bosom, lacking as it did any significant support from beneath. "What did he say?" she asked, her voice ringing in the deep tone of a large bell.

"He said the Contessa was er—" The Squire rolled his eyes and continued, "engaged in ah—that is, engaged to the fellow."

"The poor dear," the lady uttered. "Do tell us more, Mr. McClintock."

Henry hid his smile under the pretense of being overcome by emotion. "The Contessa keeps her sorrows to herself, of course. But when the news came of his passing, she fell prostrate with grief. He died so young, you see." He wiped away an imaginary tear. "Long ago, when she was hardly more than a child, she suffered her first great loss the year her husband the Conte died. She abhors death. And so this second shock was all the keener felt. The Contessa stayed shut up for many months, until an old friend pleaded with her to come to London. I daresay you read in the journals of the merry life the Contessa led while living there."

"I follow the exploits of the notables," Mrs. Colley said. "The Duke of Bedford, who often resides at Woburn Abbey when not in Town for the Season, happens to be a not-too-distant neighbour of ours." She patted her wig importantly before continuing. "Though the news from Town is not as current as one would wish, I keep thoroughly informed of the comings and goings of those of renown. The Contessa's fame precedes her."

"But at what cost came that fame?" asked Henry. "She was most unhappy, even at the gayest of balls. She has come to the country to find peace. She needs quiet and clean air. The strain upon her voice, you understand."

"Then she must stay with us," stated the Squire. He puffed out his chest. "It is my opinion that she will find all that she could desire at Ivel Manor."

Mrs. Colley unfurled her fan and from behind it whispered, "I read that she left Town very suddenly. It was reported that she went to Ireland."

Aware that the real Contessa had fled to Ireland to hide her approaching confinement, Henry said, "After her nervous collapse, we spread rumours to protect her from the curious." He turned to the Squire. "Your offer is most generous, but..." He made a helpless gesture.

"Let us leave it to the Contessa to decide," said the Squire. "I daresay she would find the manor much more to her liking than a noisy inn."

As one, they looked to where Kate now stood gazing out the window upon the April viridity of the pastoral scene beyond. Henry coughed gently for her attention. She turned slowly and began to glide towards them.

The Squire was careful to emphasize his manliness as he strode across the room to usher her to a seat. "My dear Contessa," he began in a lofty tone, "m' mother and I are extending to you—and your minions—the use of our home for as long as you choose to grace us with your presence. I entreat you to accept our *humble* home as your own. Please, say that you will stay with me—with *us*, that is."

With the black veil concealing all but her lips, Kate hid an irrepressible smile behind her gloved hand. How on earth was she to keep at a distance such an obvious lecher? She stretched a hand of supplication towards her father.

"She's overcome by your generous offer," Henry murmured to the Squire and his mother.

"Then you will stay with us, Contessa?" asked Mrs. Colley. "I long to introduce you to the local gentry. Word of your arrival in the community has spread, you see. And I would like to be the one who presents you to those wishing to meet the famous Contessa D'Alessandria. Do say you will grant me that pleasure."

Kate raised her head and, mindful of her older brother's tutoring, said, "*Si, grazie*. The *signora* is most kind." She kept her voice low and well-modulated. "To pass the days in this, the most love-liest of villas, would give my heart *molta* joy." Holding out her hand to the Squire and, sitting just so, she managed to convey something titillating to him without uttering a word.

The Squire squeezed her fingers and assumed the aspect of a rooster about to crow.

"Demme!"

Kate turned in the direction of the voice. A tall man stood in the doorway with a delicate young lady on his arm. Though her features were less pronounced than his, one could not mistake the family resemblance. Their soft brown hair was so exactly the same in hue.

"Has someone a knife?" the man asked, as he led the young lady into the room. "The Squire's laced up too tight again and looks ready to burst. Those Apollo corsets are the very devil."

Mrs. Colley placed a restraining hand on her son's arm as he took a step forward, then she gave him a pointed look. "Sir Maxim," she said to the newly arrived gentleman, "how you do go on. Such a wag. You mustn't tease my dear Jethro so. Especially as you may one day call him *brother*."

At the mention of a closer kinship, the young lady paled and clung to Sir Maxim as if he were her last hope.

Kate sat forward in her chair, watching the gentleman. Her gaze was captured by the sight of a mouth that seemed to be drawn in a secret smile. To dwell upon his full lips did unsettling things to her. When the scrutiny of his bright blue eyes fell upon her, she couldn't help but smile.

Hidden by the black veil, she felt herself at an advantage and brazened out his observation of her, even giving him a thorough inspection in return. Something deep within her stretched luxuriously and began to awaken. And she knew that she wanted to attract this man's interest—by whatever device she had to employ.

Unfurling her black lace fan, Kate sat back in the enticing manner Polonius had taught her.

Mrs. Colley stood and moved, in her side to side swinging gait, to the centre of the gathering. Having thus gained their attention, she began her introductions. "Contessa, let me make you known to Sir

Maxim Wolverton, Baronet, and his sister—my dear late nephew's widow—Lucy Gillingham.'' She motioned to the young lady, who curtsied. "Sir Maxim, may I present the Contessa D'Alessandria of the Kingdom of Sardinia.'' Her voice rang with obvious pleasure. She then moved to include Henry McClintock, but she was forestalled.

"Contessa?'' Sir Maxim gazed at Kate in surprise. He left his sister and stepped closer to her. With a marked appearance of scepticism, he leaned in to gain a glimpse of her through the veiling. *"Cara mia?* Sophia, what the deuce are you doing here in the country?''

Henry stepped hastily forward. "The Contessa is rusticating.'' He stood between Kate and her inquisitor.

"Who the devil are you?'' Sir Maxim looked at the older man with curiosity.

"Henry McClintock,'' Henry said, bowing, "late of the Royal Italian Opera House, but at present I serve as the Contessa's manager.''

Sir Maxim's brows rose and he peered round the older gentleman's shoulder to glance at Kate. His smile deepened, revealing a pair of dimples.

"I thought you knew everyone in town,'' Mrs. Colley remarked to Sir Maxim. "How could you fail to have recognized the famous songstress, the Contessa D'Alessandria?''

"How indeed?'' Sir Maxim moved around Henry to stand beside the Contessa. He took her black-gloved hand and kissed it, then held it for far too long. *"Mi scusi, cara mia,* I had not expected to find such a pleasant surprise in the wilds of Bedfordshire. How remiss of me." He caressed the back of her hand with his thumb.

Kate withdrew from his touch. Raising her head to meet his gaze, she felt the black veiling against her cheeks, perhaps revealing more of her face than she wished. She watched him for a moment, wondering. *He knows,* she realized.

Her regard was met by his quizzical stare. She smiled in a manner that indicated they shared a secret.

"It's my opinion," said the Squire, "that *Sir* Maxim doesn't know half as much as he thinks he does." He bristled with self-importance. "I daresay, sir, you'll get an education here in Bedfordshire."

"I make no doubt of it." Sir Maxim didn't bother to address the Squire, but kept his gaze trained on Kate. "Shall you be staying here for very long, Contessa?"

Henry again intervened on her behalf. "Only until we—she makes a recovery."

"That should be long enough for us to renew our friendship," remarked Sir Maxim. "Shouldn't it, Contessa?"

Kate wanted to laugh aloud. Instead, she fluttered her fan, using it with alluring effect—all the while speculating upon just what sort of friendship they were supposed to have had. This was becoming a unwonted mare's nest.

The Squire loomed over her, taking up a possessive position at her side. He glared at Sir Maxim. "The lady is under my protection, that is, she is my guest...and m' mother's," he added as an after-thought.

"As the Contessa's manager," Henry said, sensing that the scene was getting out of hand, "I must insist that she rest now. I can see that she is quite over-come—" he paused to glance pointedly at the two gentlemen "—with fatigue. We shall retire now to the inn, and return tomorrow."

"I must insist," said the Squire, "that the Con-tessa remains here."

"The inn—being a posting house—is bound to be quite noisy at this time of day," Mrs. Colley said. She gave her son a look which indicated he should be si-lent. "I'll have the housekeeper ready the Contessa's chambers—the Madame de Pompadour Rooms. I daresay, Contessa, that you'll be quite comfortable there...being a foreigner and all. Meanwhile, you shall rest in my boudoir." With the aid of her obliging hoop, Mrs. Colley wedged her way through the press of gentlemen to take her honoured guest by the hand.

"Grazie," Kate murmured as she rose from her chair. She turned to the Squire and held out her other hand in a grand gesture. *"Buona sera, Signore.* You are *molto* generous to offer us the use of your villa." She let him kiss her hand.

To her father, Kate gave a nod, indicating his suc-cess.

Behind the swinging hoop of her hostess, she fol-lowed until she reached the doorway. There, Sir Maxim waited for her. Evidently he was a man of ac-tion and forethought.

"Rest peacefully," he said, then added in a lowered tone, "As I remember, you *relax* best when in someone's arms. Alas, it appears that I must forsake that pleasure... for now."

CHAPTER TWO

SIR MAXIM STOOD in the doorway of the Grand Salon, watching the lady trimmed in black follow Mrs. Colley up the stairs. Smiling to himself, he marvelled at how unruffled the young woman had remained after his outrageous remark. If he'd been able to see her eyes he doubted whether she would have even blinked. What kind of woman was she?

As a scholar of sorts, he found himself always looking for answers. His mind was rarely idle. Even in his sleep, he suspected that some part of him went on thinking through the night, for most mornings he awoke with a myriad of new ideas and questions. Of all things, he could not endure an unanswered question.

There was order in the universe, and to discover the unknown, one only had to go methodically about with an observant eye and a receptive mind. An inquisitive disposition made life a constant education. And the mysterious lady was a subject he wanted to study.

Mentally, he began to compile a list of questions concerning her. Who was she; what was her name? She certainly wasn't the Contessa D'Alessandria. What did she look like beneath the veil? What were the colour of her eyes—true blue or cunning green? For

24 A MERRY GO-AROUND

what purpose was this impostor in Bedfordshire? Why did she smile so delightfully at the most outrageous things?

"Max!"

Sir Maxim snapped out of his reverie. He glanced across the room to see what sort of trouble his sister was in—now. Henry McClintock was nowhere in sight, but it was plain to see that the Squire was making Lucy dashed uncomfortable.

"Jethro," Sir Maxim called, crossing the room, "come, tell us all about the Contessa. You sly fox, where have you been hiding her?" He clapped the Squire upon the shoulder and pulled the fellow away from his sister. "Lucy, you shameless scamp, this sort of talk is hardly for your ears. Run along, my dear."

Lucy fled without a backward glance. Her lavender gown fluttered from the speed of her departure.

"Now that we're alone—man to man," Maxim said, "tell me all about the charming Contessa. Is she still as delightfully forthright as I remember? She seems changed."

The Squire glanced up at the ceiling and coughed. "She's in mourning for a *particular* friend. Hasn't said more than a handful of words since she got here." He sighed. "She's a rare bit of muslin, though."

Maxim gazed speculatively at the Squire. Perhaps the fellow could be diverted from lavishing his unwanted attentions upon Lucy. "Then she's still a striking beauty? I hope she hasn't lost her passionate zest for living. Mourning can be so taxing, especially for one with that burning verve so characteristic of women from the Mediterranean region." Maxim gave

Jethro the sort of look men share when they speak of spirited women. "Tell me, as a man of the world, what is your opinion of the Contessa?"

"You want my opinion?" The Squire appeared surprised, but pleased. He thrust out his chest and rocked importantly on his heels. "It is my opinion," he said in a sonorous voice, "that I've yet to see a woman with a better figure. The Contessa is a diamond of the first water."

"You've a keen eye. She is a diamond, one worth possessing. There is an aura of mystery about her which makes her all the more desirable. No doubt behind that veil there are secrets that merit exploration. But I daresay she's taken you into her confidence. What *do* you know of the Contessa?"

The Squire gave Maxim a condescending smile and waved his hand airily. "She is the Contessa D'Alessandria. What more do I need to know?"

"What indeed."

"Besides, the best way to know a woman is in the Biblical sense." The Squire leered.

Maxim felt a twinge of conscience for encouraging the lout. The Squire was no gentleman where women were concerned. "Beware, lest the wrath of the Almighty be visited upon you."

"Oh, no fear there. M' mother never finds out about my affairs of amorous congress."

"How providential."

"As head of m' family, I reign supreme. I'll not be ruled by a petticoat!" He was proud of his boast.

Longing to take the wind from the Squire's sails, Maxim said, "I would hazard a guess that the Contessa is one petticoat used to having her own way."

"Maybe so, but I haven't yet had *my* way with her. Once she's had a taste of Jethro Gillingham Colley, she'll be most obliging."

The Squire found that the Contessa was not so accommodating as he would want her to be. For days she stayed in her chamber, resting. The only ones permitted entrance were her personal maid and her family, known to those at the manor as her hirelings.

Finally, the Contessa was ready to receive company. And Mrs. Colley saw that she had plenty of it by inviting twenty or so of the most interesting people of the community to dinner and a reception with music.

In her ornate salon filled with guests, all awaiting the appearance of the Contessa, Mrs. Colley sat in a state of supreme self-importance. Only one thing marred her moment: her son seemed to think himself a footman, for he would not leave his chosen place near the door. She signalled to him, indicating that he was to be a more amiable host. He obdurately retained his patient stance. She jerked her head in the direction of the group surrounding Sir Maxim, of which Lucy Gillingham was a part.

Scowling, the Squire shuffled over to engage the young lady in conversation. But, the moment the outer door opened, he hastily excused himself and hurried forward to greet the long-awaited guest of honour. He seemed to physically deflate as the expectant expression on his face gave way to a look of comic disappointment.

"Colonel Buffard," the Squire said, stepping back quickly to avoid the slice of the cane brandished by the aged veteran of the Colonial War. A goutridden foot, made huge by its wrappings, trod upon him.

"Ugh! Miserable little pup." Colonel Buffard glared at the Squire. "Get back! Make room for a man to pass. That's the trouble with these scapegraces who call themselves gentlemen... they ain't got an ounce of manners." Slapping the Squire on the backside with his cane, the Colonel called for a drink, a cushion and a stool, then huffed by and plopped down onto the nearest chair. With a flourish, he deftly retired the cane at his side in the manner of an accomplished swordsman shielding his sabre.

The Squire collared a footman and shoved him towards the Colonel. Ignoring all else, Jethro Colley again positioned himself by the door.

"'Watch ye, stand fast in the faith'—First Corinthians 16:13." A young gentleman bowed to the Squire and stepped nearer. "Are you waiting for the Contessa? I must say that I am all agog to meet her, so is the rest of the company."

The Squire glanced at the cub at his side. "Mr. Rowden, did my mother invite you tonight? I heard you were leaving for Kent to take up a rectory there."

Bellamy Rowden, late of Oxford, grinned engagingly. "I shall accept the benefice as soon as the old codger who now holds it cocks up his toes. According to my uncle, it won't be long."

"It won't be soon enough for me." Squire Colley assumed his official look, of which he availed himself whenever he acted as magistrate. "The constable tells me you've been—what is it you young whips call it—hunting the squirrel? Must be mad to drive in such a fashion. Yesterday, Miss Sayer fainted from fright when you scraped their carriage with your gig. But, most abominable of all, you've turned all around the posting signs on the roadway. A very serious offense, sir."

"Ecclesiastes 8:15—'A man hath no better thing under the sun, than to eat, and to drink, and to be merry.' A homily you practice more thoroughly than any of us." Bellamy dug his elbow into the Squire's ribs. "I hear you are felling short-heeled wenches faster than they can throw up their skirts. My dear fellow, does your mother know where you go at night?"

The breadth of the Squire's chest increased alarmingly. "I daresay all you churchmen are great gossips. But you'd best not tattle on me, sir." He smoothed the fit of his coat over his girth and tugged at the snug garment. Dismissing the young gentleman as if he were a bothersome gnat, the Squire gave up waiting in the salon and went out into the Great Hall. He glanced beyond the footmen to the main staircase. The sight he saw brought him hopping back into the room. "She's coming," he said excitedly.

The guests surged forward, trying to see beyond the doorway. Struggling to hold his place at the forefront, the Squire kept them back and, at the same time, managed to strike a manly pose.

At the top of the stairs, Kate paused. The silver gown she wore revealed more than it concealed. But she held her lace fan in a way that effectively covered her most charming attributes. She wore a longer veil over a set of Spanish combs, which not only covered her face but draped down her back most fetchingly. With her hand upon her father's arm, she was ready to descend. "I tell you, Papa, he knows."

"He may think he knows, but he isn't saying anything. Whatever his reason, we must be thankful. Sir Maxim is a dangerous fellow. Mind your step with him." Henry proceeded with her down the stairs.

Kate sighed gustily, billowing the black veil which fluttered at the end of her nose. "This is nonsensical. One doesn't cover one's face at night."

"How are these rustics to know that the veil isn't a custom of the Contessa's homeland?" Polonius asked as he trailed behind with his older brother. "While you've *rested* these last few days, we've set the stage for you. The good folk of Biggleswade are ready to embrace you, and all your foreign foibles."

"You must remain disguised," Anthony whispered as they walked across the first landing. "We cannot risk anyone challenging your bona fides. Play your part and you will not be discovered."

She managed to knock Anthony in the shin with her heel. "Much you know about it. I've a lecherous country squire dangling after me, and a baronet who's ready to make the next move in a flirtatious game to which I don't even know the rules. Papa is penniless, cheated out of everything by a peeress with no conscience." She glanced at her father. "How you could have been so gulled by that female sharp is beyond my understanding."

"My dear, I myself am baffled. It must have been her ladyship's innocent looks and, of course, the laudanum helped. Lady Durston is more devious than the devil. But, if I am successful, she'll yet get her just deserts." Henry patted Kate's hand. "There is nothing to worry about. You must know that I would never enter a game without a trick or two up my sleeve. Hush now, Katherina," he admonished as she began to speak, "the curtain is about to rise." With magnificent aplomb, he led her into the Grand Salon.

Kate faced the assembled guests with fortitude. She saw Sir Maxim moving slowly towards her. How pleasing was his appearance. He wore his dark blue tailcoat with ease, as if other things were more important than one's dress.

Before Sir Maxim could reach her, however, Squire Colley appeared at Kate's side, possessively taking her hand and placing it upon his arm. She was borne from the safe harbour of her father's presence and led among the guests. Mrs. Colley latched on to Kate's other side and swaggered about with her son. To those closest at hand, Mrs. Colley introduced the Contessa as her dearest friend.

Glancing over her shoulder, Kate wanted to be sure that Anthony was there to give her support. She hoped, as her bodyguard, he would hold back the press of people. But instead of Anthony, a trio of admirers trailed after her. Hurrying before the other two, came a redheaded gentleman with a distracted air. One gouty old gentleman hobbled along, treading on anyone who got in his way. Next to him, but not close enough to be stepped on, came a fresh-faced young man, whose demeanour seemed at odds with his clerical collar.

Kate seized the opportunity to disengage herself from her clutching hostess and the Squire as the other gentlemen seemed to desire her recognition. She smiled in her beguiling way and slowly unfurled her fan. *"Signore?"*

"Contessa." The man with the flaming mane seemed to breathe the word in when he said it. "Rufus Sayer, at your service. I have longed for this moment. To see you and behold your—your—" He looked frustrated. "Beauty is too weak a word for your—" He ran a hand through his long hair and gasped in despair.

"Move aside, you mammering wordmonger," the old gentleman bellowed, poking his stick into Rufus's back. He thrust his grizzled face close to Kate's and confided, "He's a desperate romantic with nothing to say, so I daresay that makes him a poet. The fool fancies himself as one. M' name's Colonel Buffard, but you may call me . . . Colonel Buff, my dear, dear Contessa."

Fanning the air, Kate leaned back from the strong fumes of his liquored breath.

The young cleric elbowed his way forward to bow over her hand. " 'The desire accomplished is sweet to the soul'—Proverbs 13:19. You cannot know what meeting you means to me, ma'am. I doubt anything else in life will be as grand as this very moment."

Unexpectedly Kate felt someone touch her from behind and take her arm in a firm grasp. Anthony had at last come to her rescue. She turned with a grateful smile. However, it was not her brother, but Sir Maxim who led her away from the demands of the other guests. Without a word, he left her in the company of Mrs. Colley and his sister Lucy.

Kate hardly heard what Mrs. Colley said to her. She watched Sir Maxim as he moved away and wondered what had prompted his thoughtful gesture.

Dinner was announced and, following after Sir Maxim and Mrs. Colley, Kate went in on the arm of the Squire. To her dismay she found that the Contessa's place was right next to the Squire's. For two hours she suffered through his various attempts to touch her with his knee, leg, foot or hand. These wily forays upon her virtue were concealed beneath the tablecloth. Once she wagged a finger at him in a reproving manner and he assumed the aspect of an innocent child.

Unhappily he was soon up to his old tricks. Kate's patience thinned. Towards the end of the meal, the guests were startled by a pained outcry. Kate calmly placed her fork on the table and sat back looking guilelessly about. The Squire wrapped his hand in his napkin, through which red spots seeped, and then downed a glass of wine. Dinner concluded without any further incident.

Later in the evening, when the gentlemen rejoined the ladies in the large drawing room, the Contessa was asked to sing, and, after much coaxing, she consented. Polonius, in his guise as her maestro and made up to look older, escorted her with a flourish to the pianoforte. He sat down at the keyboard and scanned a book of music. After a quick consultation with Kate, he began to play the opening chords of an English country tune.

Blessed with a good voice and some training, Kate acquitted herself very well. And when she added a bit of theatrics to her performance, she captured her audience easily.

Although it made her nervous to look into the faces of her listeners, she couldn't help singling out a few as she sang. Sir Maxim seemed surprised that she could carry a tune, but by a smile he managed to convey his encouragement. The Squire appeared to be mentally disrobing her, and she quickly diverted her gaze from the licentious gleam in his eyes. When she glanced at Anthony and her father she was surprised to see them standing on either side of the Colonel, looking as if they were all chums. The last note of the song slowly died in her throat as the Colonel wiggled his fingers at her in a friendly little wave.

Before Polonius had raised his hands from the last, lingering chord, the Colleys' guests were on their feet applauding. Kate curtsied deeply and hid behind her veil. This first taste of fanfare embarrassed her.

"Contessa," Mrs. Colley exclaimed, as she surged forward. "We must have more. Something of an operatic nature, perhaps?"

"No, no, I must forbid it," Polonius said, with just a hint of an accent. "As madame's maestro, the one who knows her voice better than even she, I cannot allow the Contessa to attempt such foolishness. No, not until she is quite herself again."

"Might we entreat her," Sir Maxim said, pushing away from the wall where he'd been leaning, "to offer us a song from her homeland?'' He slowly advanced towards Kate. ''A simple melody sung in her native tongue.'' His suggestion seemed to please the guests.

Without flinching, Kate took up the challenge. She bowed to Maxim and smiled confidently. ''Antonio,'' she called, ''come join me in a duet.''

Anthony stepped beside her. At her cue, he began to sing the first stanza of the only Italian song he knew. He held the last note of the line and Kate repeated what he'd just sung. They continued in this fashion through the song and the effect was pleasing to hear. Being brother and sister helped in the blending of their voices.

Mrs. Colley was in transports of delight over the rendition, as were all her guests—all save one. Sir Maxim's eyes twinkled wickedly. However, he did not use his hands for clapping, but instead to hold his sides. He appeared to be having a very difficult time controlling some unholy amusement that he alone enjoyed.

Kate was held in suspense as to the source of his jocularity until she was released from singing and the guests took up such diversions as cards and gossip. Dodging her trio of admirers and the Squire, Kate made her way over to Sir Maxim.

''*Signore,* you did not enjoy my song?'' she asked in the low and husky tone of the Contessa. ''The words, they were not correct?''

Maxim covered his mouth and tried to keep his shoulders from shaking. ''The words? They were...lyrical. And you said them quite correctly. I did wonder at your choice of song."

"Did you?"

He gave her a sidelong glance. "The song is quite old and its message is timeless. The refrain is especially moving. Now, how did it go? Ah, yes, 'Oh, sailor, sailor, come back to me; I'll hug you, kiss you for a small fee. The moon is bright, we can love all night ... until the tide goes out to the sea.' The harlots of the harbour would sing it to the seamen as they sailed away." He smiled, displaying his dimples. "How well do you know Italian?"

"Quite well. It is my native tongue."

He rattled off a sentence in Italian, then grinned at her expectantly.

She looked at him in a puzzled manner. Some response seemed to be required, so she said, *"Si, grazie."*

Sir Maxim took her hand and tucked it into the crook of his arm. "You have no objection, then? A stroll in the moonlight would be delightful. Just the thing for a private conversation."

Outmanoeuvering the Squire, who seemed set on intercepting them, Maxim led her down the length of the drawing room and out to the terrace. Kate caught a glimpse of the astonished faces of her father and brothers just before she was pulled into the darkness. The murmur of voices in the room rose to an excited level as soon as the pair disappeared.

There was no moon. "My reputation will be ruined," Kate said tersely.

Sir Maxim chuckled in the darkness. "A woman of your renown should be long past worrying what others think of her." He leaned against the stone baluster of the terrace and watched her closely. "If you are wondering what I think of you, *cara mia,* let me tell you that you are the most alluring, captivating, talented imposter I've yet come across."

She gasped and stepped back. "*Signore,* what does this word 'impostor' mean? My English is not good."

"You speak very well. You sing very well. You move...well, you move in a manner that stirs a man's blood. *Dolce mia,* you've more natural grace than the Contessa. And you are much more clever than she. Confess, you are not the Contessa D'Alessandria."

Kate would not be so easily vanquished. "*Certamente,* I am the Contessa. You insult me with this mirthless joke of yours." She unfurled her fan and waved it quickly before her.

"Very good! You must be an actress. You are certainly an adventuress, but what could you possibly want in Bedfordshire?" He peered at her. "Who are you?" he asked, reaching up to lift her veil.

"You are a lout ... an insulting lout." She slapped his hand away before he could achieve his goal. "To call me, the Contessa D'Alessandria of the Kingdom of Sardinia, an adventuress—this is intolerable." She took a proud stance, one which dared him to gainsay her.

"I can prove quite easily that you are not who you say you are." He moved closer to her and put a hand on her waist. "The real Contessa has a mole, and I know where it is to be found."

Kate thrust her fan up between their faces. "While I mourn there will be none of this embracing, or searching for my mole. You know where it is and I know where it is. And that is enough." She pulled away and stared at him. "No man treats the Contessa D'Alessandria like a strumpet." With a decided snap that sounded very much like a slap, she shut her fan. "I thought better of you, sir. How sad to be so disappointed."

Her bearing was aristocratic as she left him.

Maxim was about to go after her, but a whiff of tobacco smoke stayed him. He looked around. From out of the darkness stepped the lady's bodyguard. The fellow bowed and began to pass by. How curious for him to be so near at hand. Surely the woman was in no danger from Maxim. He meant her no real harm. Why, then, did she need a protector? Who *was* she?

He wondered if the bodyguard was privy to much of their conversation. When he heard the fellow's chuckle as he walked away, Maxim reluctantly admitted he'd been bested, and by a woman.

CHAPTER THREE

"I MUST TELL YOU that it is a prodigious honour to have the Contessa with us," Mrs. Colley said to the circle of guests who sat around her. "You cannot know what a joy it is to be on such close terms with that great lady. I daresay I am the envy of the neighbourhood. And who can wonder at—" She stopped in midsentence when she saw the Contessa return alone to the drawing room from the terrace. The foreign lady's posture and swift step told their own story.

Mrs. Colley's listeners turned as one in the direction of their hostess's stare. Again the murmur of voices rose to an excited level and peaked when finally Sir Maxim returned to the room. By a mere look from that gentleman the voices stilled abruptly.

Mrs. Colley frowned when she saw her son approach the Contessa and pay special court to the lady. It was all very well to have the famous Contessa as a guest, but it would never do to have one's son ensnared by the woman—especially when he was practically promised to another. Mrs. Colley glanced at the occupant of the chair placed closest at hand and smiled fondly upon Lucy Gillingham. She was such a treasure, one that Mrs. Colley guarded jealously from any who would spirit her away. A marriage between

Jethro and Lucy would bind the girl permanently to
Ivel Manor.

In Mrs. Colley's estimation, Lucy was like a living
shrine to her dear, departed nephew, James Gillingham. And dearest James—so clever, brave and
refined—had been the link that kept Penelope Colley
connected to the world of her youth. She'd lost James,
but she would never let go of Lucy.

Though Sir Maxim had recently come to take Lucy
back to his home in Buckinghamshire, Mrs. Colley
hoped she might manage to delay their departure, just
as she had so often in the past when Lucy tried to
leave. But the dear girl's brother was a man with a
sense of purpose. Perhaps he could be distracted by a
flirtation with the Contessa, which would give Jethro
sufficient time to propose to Lucy—he'd dawdled
enough already.

Mrs. Colley's reverie ceased when she noticed the
hushed whispers about her. Across the room a startling dramaturgy began to unfold. Sir Maxim approached the Contessa, who snapped open her fan and
murmured a few words to him from behind it. He began to bow, looking as if he would go away, when
Jethro stepped between the baronet and the Contessa.

Puffing up like a fighting cock, Jethro vociferously
expressed his opinion. "The lady don't care for a certain gentleman's company...and that certain gentleman should not poach on another man's property. If
you take my meaning, sir."

With imperious deliberation, Mrs. Colley summoned her son. He strutted over, bringing the Contessa along with him.

The Squire saw that the lady was seated. Bestowing the sort of attention a shopkeeper would upon the nobility, he tried to divine her every wish before it became a desire. Could he fetch her a shawl? A glass of wine, perhaps? A cushion?

"Jethro!" Mrs. Colley's tone was that of a parent to an obstreperous child. "Do be still. I daresay the Contessa has had enough attention showered upon her for one night. There are others who require your attendance." She looked meaningfully at Lucy.

The Squire swelled his chest, as if he were about to say something, but instead he clamped his mouth shut and took on a stubborn mien. His stance was like that of a pouty little boy.

Assessing the situation, Kate rose and said, "*Scusi,* Signora Colley, but, if you would permit, I wish to retire."

In an instant, Henry and her brothers were at her side with exclaims of concern. They ushered her out, allowing her to cast one last soulful glance to the room at large before she withdrew.

Although the guest of honour was no longer among their number, the assembled company stayed on and their enjoyment of the evening heightened. For now they could discuss the Contessa freely and there was nothing that escaped their notice or appraisal.

But the guests were not the only ones reviewing the evening. Above stairs, the McClintocks were gathered in Kate's room.

"As a whole, Katherina," Henry said, "your performance lacked the assurance I would like to see from one with such a major role. You must convey that you *are* the Contessa D'Alessandria."

"She did quite well when she gave a private performance for Sir Maxim," Anthony remarked.

Kate blushed. "You were there?" she asked him in a stricken voice. "how humiliating! Am I to be watched every minute?"

"Now, now, my dear, none of these missish airs." Henry frowned at her. "What did occur out there on the terrace? I was quite surprised that you used such poor judgement. At all times you must be in control of the situation. Playing the lead means *taking* the lead, my dear."

"Apparently Sir Maxim thinks he is also cast in the part of a prime player," she retorted. "He had me outside before I could even begin to feign a swoon to stay him. But I very much doubt that my stratagem would have done the trick. He would have whisked me outside, saying a breath of air is just what I needed. He seemed intent upon his purpose."

"And his purpose was?" her father asked, a sharp edge in his voice.

Anthony chuckled. "It is too late now, Papa, to worry about the vixen after you've let her loose among the pack of wolves." He bowed to his sister. "The lady's performance was excellent. Her closing speech was magnificent. 'I thought better of you, sir. How sad to be so disappointed.'" He clapped enthusiastically. "Never saw a fellow so chagrined. It was a fine bit of acting she did."

Kate bowed her head. The scene flashed through her mind and she forced back a surge of emotion. That final part had not been acting. She *had* been disappointed. How could Sir Maxim think her that sort of woman?

She wasn't the Contessa, and he knew it. Underneath the veil she was a far different woman from the renowned songstress. Could he not see that she'd been gently bred—that she was lady? Yet how was a lady, posing as a courtesan, to indicate to a gentleman that only his honourable advances would be welcome? Tonight she'd fully realized the complexity of her situation. It placed her in a most disagreeable position. A variety of misconceptions might occur.

She rebuked herself for being a naive simpleton when she'd agreed to take a part in her father's plan. But then how could she have known that she would meet a particular man, one she hoped might hold her in the highest esteem?

"Katherina? Kate? Katie, my dear," Henry called, bringing her out of her thoughts. "Is something troubling you, girl?"

"I was merely thinking."

"About what? Have we overlooked some factor?"

"Papa, is it right to perpetrate such a fraud for the purpose of gaining money?"

Polonius gaped at her. "What other reason is there for it?" He turned to his father. "Sir, I must assume her strain of Puritanism comes from our mother's family. Now, Papa, I'm not truly criticizing you, but you shouldn't have married a country lass...though Mother was the best there ever was. It's just that this wholesome bent comes out in Kate at the most inopportune times."

"You are being too severe." Henry took Kate's chin in his hand and gazed down at her. "Katherina is just as she should be. But, my dear girl, how else am I to recoup our fortune? Lady Durston has used her influence to exclude me from all the clubs in Town. Even the gaming hells have barred their doors to me." He turned away with a look of frustration. "She may have cheated, but I have no proof. I must pay her ladyship fifteen thousand guineas by the close of June. I know of no means other than gaming to obtain such an amount in less than three months' time." His arms fell dejectedly to his sides.

Kate went to him and embraced him. "There now, Papa, if anyone can manage such a feat, 'tis you."

He hugged her in return. "I shall dashed well have to! All our ready is sunk in this enterprise. It's too late to draw back now."

"It is very surprising," Anthony remarked to no one in particular, "how freely folks will speak before someone they think a nobody. There's talk of plans for a bit of gaming later tonight. Just the thing to lift your spirits, sir."

"Cards?" Henry's eyes lit up expectantly.

"Probably," Anthony replied. "Once a week the gentlemen hereabouts get together—rather like a club—and do some heavy drinking and gaming."

"Is Sir Maxim to be among their number?" Kate asked.

Anthony smiled and shrugged.

"I daresay he would be," observed Polonius. "It's said that the fellow's a vast property holder and can well afford deep play."

Kate locked her arm through her father's and led him away from her brothers. "Dearest Papa, you won't take all their money, will you?"

He patted her hand. "My dear, there is much you've yet to learn about the world. A wise man does not fleece his flock of all their wool. He leaves enough for them to be comfortable and lets them graze in rich pastures, for he knows that another season will come when he must shear again."

"Did Mama teach you that?"

Henry's expression softened. "She was the best thing ever to come my way. I hope you'll make such a difference in a man's life someday." He sighed. "With a bit of luck, I'll have enough to give you a proper dowry. A woman should never go into marriage empty-handed."

"Or empty-hearted . . . or empty-headed," she added. "But even with a dowry, who would want to wed me? Colonel Buffard? Or the poet? Perhaps the Squire?"

"I can say with a surety that the Colonel will do you no harm. He merely enjoys teasing females. Now, the Squire's intentions are strictly dishonourable. Keep him dangling at a distance and you'll not be troubled. The Squire is the sort who makes a loud noise, but hasn't the marrow to make a real man. He'll not do for you." Henry looked thoughtful. "Someday a man will come along and he'll be worth the waiting for. And my Katherina will become *his* Katherina, and life will change.'' He cleared his throat and muttered to himself about becoming old and maudlin. Quickly kissing Kate's forehead, he left her to consult with his sons about the upcoming game.

A talented cardplayer herself, Kate wandered over to listen to their plotting. But her mind kept wandering to a knave of hearts with a secret smile and dimples.

SIR MAXIM GRINNED at his sister as he escorted her to her room. He moved her candlestick back and forth to light the shadowed recesses of the corridor. ''No sign of the Squire as yet,'' he said, easing her tight hold on his coat. ''Now that the Contessa has emerged from her rooms, I doubt you shall be troubled too greatly by him. He's bound to be occupied night and day with his pursuit of her.''

''You don't sound pleased about the Squire's interest in the Contessa,'' Lucy remarked gently. ''Could it be that she has captivated you, too, Max?''

''My purposes in seeking her company aren't as crass or lecherous as our host's. She makes a fascinating subject. I've a mind to study her.''

Lucy glanced quizzically at him. ''Study her? But you took her out to the terrace. And there was no moonlight. Everyone thought the most shocking things were occurring. I could tell that the Squire wanted to intrude, but he seemed hesitant to do so. He's afraid of you. Which is why I was quite surprised when he pressed his advances on me last night.''

"You've been bothered by the lout long enough. I should get you home without further delay. Would you care to leave tomorrow or the day after?"

"Max, you cannot want to go now!" She looked up and down the corridor before continuing in a whisper. "After I've suffered weeks of boredom here, finally something provocative occurs with the Contessa's coming and you mean to leave in the midst of it all. What infamy!"

"But I thought you feared that the Squire might make you an offer?" Maxim glared down at her. "I came here posthaste at your bidding to take you away from such a misfortune. Now, you are telling me you *want* to stay?"

Lucy lowered her head, shamefaced. "Life's at last becoming more interesting. It's been dreadfully dull mourning James. I thought the year would go on forever. You were right, Max, I should never have married a man I'd known so short a time. It was all over so quickly—wed one moment and widowed the next." A tear slid down her cheek. "But I don't think I ever loved him. He just seemed to need me."

"I must get you away from here," Maxim said sternly.

She shook her head. "Then you would be actually doing me a disservice. I'm coming to realize that I need to stand for myself without leaning so much on others. Ivel Manor is an ideal place to build my self-determination. If I can withstand Mrs. Colley's machinations and her son's foolishness, then I know I shall be fit to go out in the world on my own. Besides, you would be close by to save me should I falter too badly, and you would have an opportunity to 'study' the Contessa.''

"If you desire to stay on, we shall do so." He chucked her under the chin. "I can see already that you are fast becoming a lady who knows her own mind, one who will not suffer being told what to do."

"I can see that you need to study more about my gentle sex," she retorted. "And the Contessa will make a fine lesson for you." She pecked him on the cheek and bid him a good night.

Left alone with his thoughts, Maxim wondered if he would ever be allowed to further his knowledge of the sham Contessa. He thought perhaps he should discover whether she would receive him or not. With this in mind, he started back down the corridor, away from his allotted bedchamber.

But in an alcove just beyond her rooms, he stood considering what he should do. He wanted to apologize for his boorish behaviour, but creeping into the spurious Contessa's bedchamber on the sly hardly seemed conducive to his purpose. Besides, it was late. The only guests who lingered were those intent upon gaming. At such an irregular hour, she would think he was making another improper advance rather than trying to make amends.

Yet how was he to proceed with his purpose while tripping over a house full of people? He would have to devise opportunities to be alone with the lady. If he wanted to find out all that he needed to know about her, he would have to outwit the entire lot. He'd give a hundred pounds just to know her name; however, one of the joys of acquiring knowledge was the quest.

Denying himself the pleasure of the pursuit was something he would not do.

She was a challenge, and he vowed he'd not be bested again.

At the opening of a door, Maxim drew back into the shadows. He saw Mr. McClintock step out into the dimly lit corridor from the Contessa's room. Maxim's brow wrinkled as he wondered why that gentleman should be keeping such late hours in the supposed Contessa's chamber. Surely the fellow was too old for her. Did she favour the settled, elderly sort?

McClintock's happy step indicated he was well satisfied. He even whistled as he went down the hallway and took the stairs.

An irrational wave of disappointment washed over Maxim. He'd thought better of her. He might have treated her less than honourably, but he would never have taken advantage of her. Something about the way she stiffened when he put his hand to her waist told him that she wasn't accustomed to being handled in such a manner. But here was evidence to the contrary.

Only moments after Mr. McClintock's exit, the door opened again. The maestro slipped out, looked this way and that, then crept away to the stairs.

Maxim's lips pressed tight together and his jaw set, showing his riled state of mind. What the blazes was she doing in that room?

Before he could form an answer, the door once more swung open and this time Antonio, the bodyguard, came out. He stood for a moment in the doorway. He said something indistinguishable, but obviously provocative, for the fraudulent Contessa laughingly came to him and embraced him.

The fellow's broad shoulders kept Maxim from seeing the uncovered face of the lady. Maxim was tempted to disclose his presence and confront her. But that didn't seem very sportsmanlike. Besides, his questions would likely go unanswered, and that he couldn't bear.

"Tony," she said, as she moved back into the room, "be sure that he doesn't play too deep. I would be most unhappy if he should—"

Maxim tried to lean forward to catch her words. Did she say if he should be ruined, or if he should ruin someone? And who was *he*? Maxim stirred with growing ire.

Before retreating down the corridor, the bodyguard paused to look about and listen. Maxim pulled back when the fellow turned in his direction. Then, shrugging, Antonio went away.

Maxim stepped out of the alcove and stood with his hands on his hips. What sort of game was this female playing? Men parading out of her bedchamber at such an ungodly hour! Here was the most unseemly display of lewd behaviour he'd ever witnessed. Then he smiled begrudgingly. Well, perhaps not the most.

Reluctantly, he admitted to being perplexed. Instead of learning more about this young woman, he found himself faced with even more questions. He thought for a moment. Directness had been met with evasion. Thus a circuitous course was required to achieve his goal. He would approach her through her minions, and he would begin with her manager.

A diabolical gleam lurked in his blue eyes as he paused before her door to bow, then he slipped down the hall and took the stairs with a purposeful stride.

He found Mr. McClintock in the Squire's library with the gentlemen who'd stayed to do some gaming. The genial manager was in the middle of a story about the Contessa. His attentive audience listened with wide eyes and an assortment of randy grins.

Maxim was surprised to hear that it was an actual account of one of the real Contessa's bawdier exploits when she appeared on stage in flesh-coloured tights and fig leaves. The licentious tale seemed to whet the appetites of the listeners. Though the wine flowed freely, the teller of the tale did not drink, but only held his cup of strong punch.

By the time Mr. McClintock finished with his embellishment the Squire was breathing heavily and looking odd. He sat down stiffly at the gaming table and drank deeply until his large tankard of punch was emptied. "What a woman! And I, my friends, have first claim on her."

"I ain't seen a *JGC* on her, not yet," snapped Colonel Buffard.

"Well, she's staying in my house," retorted the Squire.

The young cleric, Mr. Rowden, strolled up to the round gaming table. "Ah, yes! And 'blessed are they which do hunger and thirst after—'" he raised his brows comically and smirked "—ah, '*righteousness*: for they shall be filled'—Matthew 5:6." He sauntered around the table, out of striking distance from the Squire. "Besides, she's your mother's guest, remember? I wonder if your mother knows just what you have in mind for the Contessa's entertainment.''

The Squire reared up in his chair, but the Colonel knocked him back in his seat with his cane, saying, ''You may have stolen the march on us, Squire Jethro Gillingham Colley, but the prize ain't yet yours to claim. She's a fine-looking female—as fine as any I've seen in all my days—and until she gives one of us that particular look she's fair game.'' The Colonel's expression softened, as he seemed to gaze off at a place only he could see. ''The Contessa reminds me of a woman I knew long ago. She was our Lady of the May for several years. Now, she was a woman who had a way with the men.'' He clicked his tongue and sighed.

''Well, this year, when I'm the winning captain of our upcoming cricket match,'' the Squire said, tipping back in his chair, ''I'll be the one who chooses the Lady of the May.''

''It's a damned affront to all the good women hereabouts,'' said the Colonel. ''Last year when you presided over the May Day festivities in such unlordly fashion, we town fathers had the deuce of a time squelching the ensuing scandal.'' He glared at the Squire. ''Many a young maid had to leave the village in disgrace. I was told the list of parish foundlings increased by seven this year due to your rutting ways. You, the Lord of the May? Faugh! Never, you miserable scapegrace.''

The Squire preened importantly. ''Colonel, there is none better than I.'' He smiled in a self-satisfied manner. ''It is my opinion that your Ickwell Green team doesn't stand a ghost of a chance against my

Biggleswade boys. I recommend your village not even show for the cricket match. Just send the prize money over and I'll see that my lads get their fair share. 'Twould be a disgrace if you did play.''

"Only b'cause you stole our best bowler," retorted the Colonel, "and set him up as your tenant farmer. I call that very unsportsmanlike conduct." He glared at the Squire. "Comes close to cheating."

The Squire's chair fell back with a crash as he lunged to his feet. "Cheating! You sorry old bag of bones, you're just fuming because no one will champion your team of losers. You couldn't find a patron for that sorry bunch of grave-markers, much less a captain to lead them." He took out a pouch and dumped the contents on the gaming table. "I wager this pile of guineas that you can't find anyone to head your team."

"Then you lose," a quiet, but firm voice said.

CHAPTER FOUR

THE GENTLEMEN in the Squire's library turned and stared at Sir Maxim. But it was the Squire himself who appeared the most stunned by what his guest had just said.

For a moment their host looked like the village idiot with his mouth gaping open and his eyes bulging with surprise. He recovered, struck a pose and asked, "What do you mean, sir, by saying I lose?"

"I daresay my meaning is evident," Sir Maxim said, taking a seat and leaning back at his ease. Then he added quietly, "Even to a simpleton. But for you, Squire, I will expound upon the subject. You offered a small wager to Colonel Buffard. You have lost that wager. Why? Because the Colonel has a captain for his team and a patron to support them." He turned his gaze upon the Colonel. "And I am that man if he'll have me."

"My dear sir," exclaimed the Colonel, looking as merry as a child with a new toy, "I gladly accept such a generous offer. I'm handy at instructing swordplay, but I've no talent for cricket. You're a demmed godsend, sir—no mistake about it!" Under the Squire's seething regard, he picked up the guineas one by one and dropped them into his cupped palm. At the last satisfying clink of coin against coin, he sighed rapturously. "May not have been the biggest bet I've ever won, but it was the best."

The Squire glared at Maxim. "Demmed impudence. You're a guest in my house. If you wanted to play, I'd have given you a place on my team."

"Ah, there's the rub. I've no need to become one of your tenant farmers, don't you know." Touching his fingertips together, steeple-fashion, Maxim watched his host nearly have an apoplectic fit, turning red in the face and gasping for air. "My dear fellow, no need to take on so. It's only a cricket match."

Henry McClintock stepped into the breech. "With two such captains, it is bound to be the best game ever played in these parts."

"The blacklegs will have a rare time of it," observed Bellamy Rowden.

"Huh?" One of the locals looked confused.

"He said the bookmakers will be quite busy," explained Henry, kindly sharing a little of his vast knowledge of all aspects of gaming.

The Colonel poked his cane into the Squire's side, giving him a good jab. "I'll make you a grown man's wager. Here's my note for a hundred pounds, young Jackanapes, which I wager on the outcome of the match. Of course I favour Ickwell Green."

"A hundred!" Young Mr. Rowden looked surprised. "I say, sir, you must be confident to stake that amount—being as you are a pensioned officer and a known muckworm when the offering plate is passed on Sundays."

"I may not flash my blunt like a common Cit," the Colonel retorted, looking about at the trappings in the room. "But my kin were kind enough to die and leave me well-off. To a tithe-stealin' churchman I may be a muckworm, but to those who matter I'm thought to be a right clever investor."

Agilely side stepping the swinging cane, Mr. Rowden glanced at the Squire and grinned. "And what about you, sir? Do you think your mother would approve of you making such a bet? Proverbs 1:8—'Forsake not the law of thy mother.'"

The Squire's chest swelled alarmingly. "I am a man full grown. I am master in my house. I accept Buffard's wager and I offer him odds of two to one." He rocked on his heels and raised his head in an attitude of supreme smugness.

Bellamy Rowden snorted disdainfully. "Must not think much of your chances to offer such paltry odds."

"Damn your impudence! Three to one, and let no man say those ain't handsome odds."

The young cleric glanced away, muttering a rude remark.

"Gentlemen, gentlemen," said Henry McClintock in a placating tone, "shall we save this gaming fervour for the play before us. Come, have some drink, Squire. No doubt, you hold the bank—being as you are one of the most prosperous men in the community, you can afford to cover the wagers. Besides, one can tell by your bold approach that you are a man who could boast of his skill at any game of chance." He glanced down at the dicing box resting on the table and a disappointed sigh escaped him. Then with his usual geniality, he said, "Shall we all be seated and begin?"

The chosen amusement, a dice game called *Passe-dix*, proved to heighten the competition between the men. From the very first shake of the die box, the Squire and Sir Maxim waged a private battle, with the Colonel giving his new patron flank support. Maxim staked a notable amount against the Squire's ability to throw less than ten. The Colonel promptly backed the wager with his stack of guineas. The three dice were cast and came to rest on the baize-covered table.

"Fifteen!" crowed the Colonel. "You've rolled above a ten. Pay up, Squire, and throw again."

Squire Colley marked a note for each of the winners, doubling their original stake. Picking up the dice, he glanced about, seeming to dare anyone to bet against him. He failed to daunt them. When he spilled out the dice and they rolled to a stop, Bellamy Rowden and Henry McClintock joined the list of winners.

Yet it was Sir Maxim that the Squire singled out as his foe. And so fierce became the conflict between the two men that they failed to notice that Henry McClintock was steadily amassing considerable winnings.

It wasn't long before the Squire assumed a glowering mien, having consumed a ruinous amount of drink. As holder of the bank, he was losing at the rate of a hundred guineas per large gulp of strong spirits. Any number ten or below seemed to elude him when he tossed the dice. Soon sullenness gave way to reckless abandon.

After a period of losing much more than he won, the Squire called for another set of the ivories, but to no avail. Finally he passed the box of dice to another. Henry bravely offered to see if he could shake the bones loose to favour the thrower with a low number.

Sir Maxim pushed away from the table, refusing to bet for several casts. After all, he hardly considered himself a gamester. That he chose to play at all went counter to his usual habits.

He observed the game and its players. Mr. Mc-Clintock displayed an expert turn of the wrist when he tipped over the box. The dice repeatedly fell in his favour. They seemed to know they were in the hands of a master.

Some of the winnings that the Colonel and the others had taken from the Squire now came into the hands of Mr. McClintock. Yet Maxim could detect no irregularities in his gaming. He was a gracious victor and a wise player. He never won so much as to discourage the company.

After a time Sir Maxim thought he had the measure of the man—a sharp among flats. But when the Squire sank under the table in a drunken stupor, Mr. McClintock called a halt and, with the finesse of the finest of gentlemen, he persuaded the locals to end the play for the night. A reckoning was made and the accounts were settled, except for the Squire's.

The men departed in the best of spirits, for the Contessa's manager had promised that the songstress would be receiving guests. He also gained permission to stand as banker for a Faro table at the next gathering. Since Faro was considered a game for the aristocracy, the countrified gamesters thought they were in for a rare treat.

Had they seen, as Sir Maxim did, the gleam in Mr. McClintock's eyes, they might not have been quite so jovial.

When the older gentleman came back from ushering the remaining guests out, Maxim was not surprised to see him whistling and stepping lightly, as if doing a little jig. Turning away in disgust, Maxim rang for a servant to help the Squire to bed, but no one answered the summons.

From the corner of his eye, he saw Mr. McClintock quickly add the total of the notes the Squire had signed. The fellow tapped his finger upon his lip, looking thoughtful, then he crumpled up a couple of the notes and tossed them into the fire. Almost as an afterthought, he destroyed one more.

Perplexed, and having no desire to be caught spying, Maxim strolled over to a sideboard and poured himself a glass of wine. He winced when he took a sip— port. He'd never acquired a taste for its sweet, full-bodied richness. That he'd not given a thought to what he was doing just showed him how distracted he'd been by Henry McClintock's strange behaviour.

Why the devil would he burn the notes? It was quite out of character for a gaming sharp. Maxim knew he needed to learn more about the fellow.

"Mr. McClintock," Maxim called, "won't you come and join me in one last drink before retiring?" He refrained from saying that the gentleman was suspiciously sober after a night which had been one of deep imbibing.

The older gentleman crossed the room, glancing briefly at the slumbering figure of the Squire under the table. "The young bucks these days don't seem to have much of a head for convivial company. Rather rag-mannered with the ladies, too. I cannot like the way the Squire lusts after the Contessa." He shook his head. "Most unseemly."

"You appear to take a particular interest in the welfare of the Contessa, above that of a mere manager."

"We've known each other for quite some time. I take a fatherly interest in her affairs," Mr. McClintock said with a smile. "And standing as I do as the lady's protector, of sorts, I must comment upon the very familiar attitude that you have towards her. I daresay you once knew her quite well."

"We've been on close terms," said Maxim, as he caressed the side of his glass. "Which is why I am puzzled by her distant attitude. A *real* Contessa would not treat her friends so shabbily."

"A true lady would never tolerate presumptuous behaviour. Amorous liaisons must be discreetly conducted."

The memory of seeing Mr. McClintock slip out of a particular lady's room passed through Maxim's mind. He frowned. "Some women are fickle, letting any man come and go at will. Old goats or young bucks, it matters not. Yet this same wilful female keeps others at a distance."

"If the Contessa seems unapproachable, perhaps it is because she is overtired. She's been greatly tried of late. The strain of constantly performing has taken its toll. May I offer some advice?"

"If you must."

Henry McClintock held his affability even in the face of Maxim's daunting aspect. "As a man, older and wiser, I advise you to temper your desires while you and the Contessa continue at Ivel Manor. Perhaps a rendezvous might be arranged for a later time, after our visit here has ended. Would you like me to convey your invitation to the Contessa?"

"Anything that passes between the Contessa and myself shall be of a private nature. No man does my wooing for me. But it was generous of you to offer, considering your own close attachment to the lady."

The older gentleman's brows rose in astonishment. "My affection for her is wholly paternal, sir. And I'll knock down any man who dares to besmirch the fine character of that dear, virtuous girl."

"Virtuous? Are we speaking of the same notorious courtesan? She is the Contessa D'Alessandria, is she not?" Maxim scrutinized Henry McClintock with a look of cynicism. The gentleman appeared flustered, as if caught out of character.

"Satire, sir. I was using it to show how ludicrous your assumption was. Yet I cannot help being protective of the dear lady. She reminds me very much of my own daughter—Katherina." Henry pulled out his timepiece, then yawned stagily. "How late it has become. I daresay the servants are fast asleep. Dare we attempt to carry the Squire up to his room?"

Maxim eyed the great bulk that reposed under the table. "Though a blatherskite full of his own importance, the Squire is a bruiser I'd as lief not try to haul up the stairs. We might be able to lift him onto the sofa.''

After a great deal of heave-hoing, the deed was done and the two gentlemen went up to bed. Each was quietly lost in his own thoughts.

''What is the colour of your daughter's eyes?'' Sir Maxim asked, as they reached the top of the stairs. ''Are they green or blue or...?''

Henry chuckled in a sleepy manner. ''Why, they are similar in colour to the Contessa's. Only Katherina's eyes are much more pure and richer in hue.'' He bid Maxim a goodnight and retired to the small room allotted to him.

The fellow was a slippery eel, Maxim thought. Henry McClintock might be the lady's protector, but did that make him her lover, or father, or just what? She couldn't be his daughter. That obvious slip of information had surely been given to lead him from the truth. But if McClintock's hint had been genuine, why had he given it? What could he hope to gain by making such a revelation?

Maxim clenched his jaw. More questions and no answers, as yet. He still needed to come up with a first-rate plan, one that would outwit a clever adventuress and her accomplices.

An idea with great appeal began to germinate in his mind. His contemplations brought that secret smile to his lips. He hoped Lucy hadn't misjudged her ability to stay longer, since he intended to remain until the last player's true character was unveiled.

To accomplish this end, Maxim would need to use all the cunning he possessed and every advantage at his command. Perhaps even the Squire could be handled as a tool in the proper circumstances.

The notion of taking advantage of the neighbourhood bully did not trouble Maxim one whit. The cocksure Jethro Gillingham Colley might find a few surprises in the days ahead which would leave him with little to crow about. On that happy thought, Sir Maxim retired for the night a few hours before dawn.

LATER THAT MORNING, those who were still asleep were jarred awake by a commotion coming from the library. The Squire, in a befuddled state, had risen and availed himself of what he thought to be his chamber pot. A maid entered the library with dust-bucket in hand and began caterwauling at the sight of the Squire poised by a Grecian urn. He resembled a lewd water-fountain Cupid.

After this unpropitious beginning, the day did not improve for the Squire. Hardly had he retreated to his bed, before his man was shaking him awake. Upon hearing that Colonel Buffard awaited him belowstairs in the library to discuss an urgent matter, the Squire began to swear soundly. But he stopped before he completely uttered the first syllable. He clutched his head, rolled his eyes and moaned. Throughout his haphazard toilette he whined and whimpered.

He eased down the stairs as if he were made of glass. When a footman sprang to open the library door, he motioned for quiet since the slightest sound threatened to shatter his nerves.

"Buffard," the Squire whispered in a dry, rasping voice, "what is the meaning of this intrusion? Demme your impudence, pulling a man from his bed."

"Impudence!" cried the Colonel, rapping the floor with his cane. He grinned when the Squire winced and moaned. "My good man, it is all of ten o'clock. Only a sluggard is abed at this advanced hour of the day. But I'm here first because I wanted to steal the march on them all. I've come to pay a call on the Contessa."

The Squire's eyes did an odd dance in their sockets. He turned a greenish-grey colour. Clamping a hand over his mouth, he dashed about wildly. Finally he thrust his head into the same large urn he'd put to use earlier that morning and retched long and hard. Just as he was pulling his head out of the vessel the Contessa entered the room, looking as fresh and lovely as a dew-touched flower.

Kate began to advance, but stopped abruptly. She retreated several steps, raising her handkerchief to her nose. "Excuse me, Squire, I didn't know you were quite so occupied. Perhaps I should receive the Colonel in one of the drawing rooms." She hurried out.

"I'll be with you directly, my dear," called the Colonel. "But first I must tend to certain matters with the Squire." He advanced upon the hapless younger man. "No use hiding in there all day." He grabbed the Squire's shoulder and pulled him away from the urn. "Since you've cast up your accounts," he said with a relishing cackle, "it seems only proper that you pay up on what's owed. Here are your notes from last night. I've come to collect my three hundred and fifty guineas!"

"Three hundred what!" The Squire immediately regretted his sharply uttered words. He closed his eyes gently and groaned in a manner that was close to weeping.

"That's three hundred and fifty guineas," said the Colonel gleefully. "Daresay you never thought you'd have to part with so much of the ready to an old man like me. But, scapegrace, I've come to collect it all." Then seeing the Squire take on a greenish hue again, he said, "But we can settle up after I've seen the Contessa." He hobbled out.

The Squire staggered to the door after him and leaned on the frame for support. "I'll want to see every one of those notes before I hand over such an amount."

Rufus Sayer, following behind a footman, stopped short and gaped at the Squire. "Notes?" He glanced down at the sheaf of papers he carried. "You want to see the poems I've written for the Contessa? Perhaps I should read them to you, as I've done so much crossing out here and there." Before proceeding, the poet ran his hand through his red hair and cleared his throat. "I've entitled the first one *The Contessa's Hair*. 'Dark as the night/ Diamonded with stars so bright/ Soft as the gentle wind—'" He halted when the Squire threw back his head and ran for the urn. He grimaced at the retching sounds reverberating from the vessel. "Well, that is only one man's opinion."

CHAPTER FIVE

IN THE SMALL BLUE DRAWING ROOM, located in a quiet corner of the grandiose manor house, Kate sat surrounded by admirers. It seemed that a goodly portion of the male population of the district had come to pay court to the Contessa. Kate turned this way and that, trying to catch what was being said to her, as each gentleman clamoured for her attention.

When Rufus Sayer shambled into the room and proclaimed, "Contessa, behold your insignificant servant!" the others fell quiet and stared at him.

The poet Sayer staggered forward as if completing the last few steps of a long pilgrimage. "I care not what the world thinks of my verses. I humbly offer them to the only one who can judge their worth." He fell to his knees before Kate, bowed his head and extended his offering. He maintained his abject posture until she finished scanning through the sheets of paper.

"It is I who must feel humbled, *signore,* by your soul-stirring tribute." She hoped the veil would cover her blush. "No one has ever written such fine words about me."

Colonel Buffard cleared his throat loudly and frowned at Kate. "Contessa, you needn't fib for the benefit of this versifier. It's well known that there's been plenty of sonnets written praising every part of you from head to foot. This impudent puppy must think to join the others.''

"I daresay," Kate murmured, "that Signore Sayer has surpassed the rest. His verses evoke a—a—how do you say it?—a poignancy which the others failed to achieve.''

Rufus Sayer grabbed her hand and and kissed it passionately. "My goddess, my all! The generosity of your words is—is—'' He ran a hand through his fiery locks and moaned. "It's more than I deserve," he uttered, then grimaced as if dissatisfied with his paltry efforts and amended his words by saying, "More than I ever dared to dream." Abruptly he stood, his hands clasped to his chest. "Your goodness of heart warrants an ode—no, an epic! Only a longer work would suit the depth of my regard and bring to light the true nobility of your inner soul. I must hie to my sanctuary for I must be alone. The muse...it is coming!" He made his exit in a style comparable to Kemble.

"Insufferable young jackanapes!" The Colonel swung his cane, scattering the Contessa's throng of admirers. The gentlemen resumed their seats, but scooted back since the Colonel appeared to be in a jousting mood with his stick.

Kate invited the Colonel to place his chair closer to hers, hoping she might spare someone the loss of his sight from a jab to the eye. Then, with the ease of a practiced courtesan, she resumed her reign over the salon, giving a word here and a look there as she kept the gallants happy. Though Anthony was close at hand, Kate, as the Contessa, had to deal with them on her own. Being the focus of every gentleman's attention was a circumstance with which she was unfamiliar.

Yet when she played the part of the Contessa, she found that flirtation and friendly banter came readily to her. It was as if by lowering the veil over her face she became another person. But she revelled in this newfound entity within her. She didn't miss the retiring, rather shy spinster who'd given up the hope of ever knowing what it was like to truly live. She felt that a hidden facet of herself had been set free; and now she couldn't restrain the ever-present smile which accompanied her new animation.

However, her smile faltered for a moment when the Colonel leaned over to present all the reasons why he would make an ideal protector for any enterprising female desirous of an illicit connection.

"I'm a man still in my prime," whispered the Colonel, sucking in the round belly it had taken him over sixty years to acquire. "I do enjoy the sport of Venus. Perhaps not with the vigour of a younger man, but I do like a bawdy banquet every week. Keeps a man young and helps him to sleep better."

Kate bit her lip. Did the Colonel say such things merely to be shocking? Having survived the conversation thus far, she was past the need to blush. But how to respond was beyond her, so she repeated something she'd overheard from her brothers. "Some believe it a better cure than being cupped."

Cackling with delight, the Colonel attracted the attention of the others in the room. Naturally the gentlemen were curious to know the cause of his mirth. He told them crossly to tend to their own affairs, then leaned a little closer to Kate and began to murmur honeyed words in her ear.

She drew back, but not knowing quite how to deal with his outrageous behaviour she soon made a game of the dalliance and included her other admirers. After a while, though, as the Colonel became more foolish, even the playacting paled. Had it not been for the ingenuity needed to carry on a successful flirtation, she would have languished from boredom. Contrary to her expectations, she discovered nothing to be more tedious than effusive compliments. Her attention wandered from the clustered gentlemen when they began to argue over whether her skin was like a dew-covered rose petal or the finest pale satin.

Kate glanced out the long windows and wished she could slip away, but her gaggle of admirers would trail after her. Next she began to count the number of *JGC*s in the room. She'd found twenty-seven when her gaze met that of Sir Maxim.

She peered at him through the veil, wondering if he knew she was watching him as intently as he watched her. He stood just inside the doorway, leaning against the wall. How long had he been there? He didn't appear desirous of joining the cluster around her, but seemed content to remain at a distance, watching.

Dispiritedly, Kate remembered their last moments together the night before. When he'd approached her in the drawing room, she'd sent him away with a few terse words.

Inwardly she groaned. She'd wanted his respect and admiration. How irrational to think that he would be different from the others and think of her in a kindly light. But she was ready to give him another chance. Surely if he stayed in her company for very long he would recognize that she was a lady.

The sudden stillness in the room called her attention away from the object of her thoughts. She looked about at the expectant faces of her admirers.

"I say, Contessa, have we offended you?" one fellow asked.

"Lout!" The Colonel rapped the unfortunate gentleman with his cane. "Never ask a lady to settle a sporting matter. It's beyond her realm of knowledge. How the devil is she to know which team is better— Ickwell Green or Biggleswade? Like asking a babe to address an issue in Parliament."

"You will come watch our Biggleswade team practice, won't you, Contessa?" someone asked.

The Colonel led the Ickwell supporters in their derisive comments on that suggestion. The men tumultuously began to take sides, placing the Contessa in the midst of their squabble.

"Gentlemen!" Kate shouted to be heard. *"Signore, fermo!"* She leapt up and grabbed the arm of one man as he raised it in anger against another. "Enough, I say! I shall visit both teams." She winced at an exchange of curses. *"Avete capito?* This unseemly behaviour is not worthy of you. And you dishonour me by your ungentlemanly conduct." Her speech had the effect she desired. The men calmed down and gradually backed away from each other. To insure their complete capitulation, she shed a tear and looked doleful.

Coming upon the scene, Henry McClintock stopped just inside the doorway and glanced about. "What is this? Gentlemen, how have you upset our dear Contessa?" He pointed to Kate, who clutched a handkerchief and sniffed audibly.

She sighed heartily. The Contessa had held court for long enough for one day. With this in mind, she said, "I came to the country for peace. All of this quarrelling has quite overset me. I feel...faint." She held the back of her hand to her forehead in an affected gesture of frailty, then, to seal the success of her performance, she swayed and began to buckle at the knees.

Fortunately, Anthony reached her side before she had to complete her swoon. The Contessa's admirers looked decidedly shamefaced and ill at ease.

"Now what?" Anthony whispered to Kate.

"Look to Papa," she murmured.

Henry strode to the centre of the room.

"Rebellious subjects, enemies to peace,
profaners of this neighbour-stained steel—
Will they not hear? What, ho! you men, you beasts,
That quench the fire of your pernicious rage—"

He paused to draw a breath.

Moaning, Kate murmured, "*Romeo and Juliet*? Help me to a chair, Tony. This is likely to be a lengthy speech."

But before Henry could continue, Bellamy Rowden bounded into the room, saying, "If any of you chaps wish to redeem the Squire's vowels he's got his strongbox open. Best hasten before he closes it."

The Colonel pushed past everyone, treading on any who got in his way. "Have some respect for the elderly," he hollered, clouting the unwary on the head. He was out the door before the rest.

Henry waited until the room was nearly empty before reaching into his waistcoat pocket and extracting several slips of paper. He winked at his two children and joined the procession to the library.

A disquieting silence settled over the three left behind in the drawing room. Looking from Sir Maxim to Kate, Anthony chuckled and said to his sister, "I shall leave you to your own devices, Contessa." He made a servile bow, then moved to a chair in a far corner of the room. Kate motioned for his return to her side. He merely grinned at her and closed his eyes as if to sleep—becoming a defunct chaperon.

Quite aware that Sir Maxim was still watching her from his place against the wall, Kate unfurled her fan and plied it slowly just before her veil. She felt rather like a mouse being considered by a tomcat. Was he going to amuse himself with her for a time, or immediately devour her?

She began to fume under his regard. "Do you never tire of holding up walls, *signore*? You Englishmen find the most, ah, curious things to do to pass the time."

Sir Maxim pushed away from where he was leaning and walked leisurely towards her. "And what do they do in Sardinia to while away the hours?"

Fluttering the fan before her, she replied in a flippant tone, "We *fare l'amore, certamente*."

"Of course," he murmured, taking the chair where the Colonel had sat so close beside her. He leaned near her. "You make love. The Contessa D'Alessandria is well known for that. But for what are you well known, my dear impostor?"

"I—I do not know what you are meaning, *signore*," she said, using a very deliberate accent to appear obtuse.

He reached over and traced the line of her lower lip. She shied from the intimate caress. "That proves it," he said, with an amused catch in his voice. "You are most assuredly not the Contessa. You are not accustomed to the ways of men. As I watched you with the others, I could see that you were not always comfortable with flirtation. You blushed once or twice. The Contessa never blushes."

"I didn't blush when the Colonel—" Kate caught herself speaking in her normal voice. She struggled to keep up her pretense. "*Signore,* cannot we be friends?"

He smiled in a knowing fashion. "Can a man and a woman be merely friends?"

"Are not you and the Contessa particular friends?—that is, are not we friends?"

"The Contessa and I are..."

His unfinished statement left Kate in a hopeless state of not knowing. "You were once my *amante. Si?*"

"No, I was never the Contessa's lover. But she wanted me. She was ready to cast off her current protector—my closest friend—if I would elope with her.

Loyalty is quite foreign to her. She is not steadfast like you."

"What do you know of me?" Kate asked, stumbling in her effort to maintain her role.

"I don't know nearly enough. I wish to know more." He smiled fully, invitingly, displaying the dimples in his cheeks. "To the folk of this little nook of Bedfordshire, you are the Contessa D'Alessandria. To me, you are a woman veiled in mystery." He leaned closer to her. His hand came up and one finger began to lift the black netting.

"Please, Signore Maxim," she murmured, pulling away from his touch. "That is not permitted." She rose from her parlour chair and moved to look out the long windows. A divergence of emotions threatened to overset her resolve to play out her part. She had to remind herself that her father's opportunity to retrieve his fortune depended upon her. With a great effort of will, she pushed her own desires aside, and then struck a pose, once again taking on her role as the Contessa.

He came up behind her, putting his hands on her shoulders. "Don't," he whispered. "Let me know *you*. If you would just raise your veil so that I might look into your eyes I know I would see a virtuous woman. I don't know why you continue with this pretense, especially with me. I don't know why you would want to be thought the Contessa or why you've come here. But I shall discover everything about you."

"I assure you, it would be a disappointment," she said, a touch of sadness in her voice, then added with spirit, *"signore."*

"Woman, you try a man's patience."

She felt him chuckle in spite of himself. Turning, she stepped back and gazed up at him. "But you are a man who is keenly aware of the sensibilities of others. You would not force me to make a revelation about myself. It is not in your nature to be unkind to those you think weaker than you."

"I dislike clouding your shining image of me, but I don't seem to be able to refrain from roasting the Squire—a thorough swine, in my opinion. So you see, I'm not always kind. Your mystic powers might be misleading you. How can you be so sure that you are reading my character correctly?" He quirked a doubting brow.

She looked down in consternation, then something sparked within her and she raised her chin regally. "You must know that the Contessa is well versed in the ways of the world. Besides, I've studied the work of Johann Lavater. His book *Essays in Physiognomy* addresses the disclosures about ones character to be found in the face, particularly the eyes. Your eyes reveal a high intellect. A questing nature." She tilted her head in a considering fashion as she gazed at him. From behind her the sunlight lit up her profile, revealing a delightful outline of her features. At his quick intake of breath, she said, "I daresay you are surprised that I know you so well."

"I am enraptured. Pray continue."

"You are a man of extraordinary stamina, possessing great fervour." She glanced down as her cheeks flushed at the thoughts engendered by her words.

"What a very fine opinion you have of me. Such an assessment must make a modest man blush." He stroked her lowered jaw. "Still, I wonder what the veil conceals about your face. Shall I have a look to see?"

With a rustle of skirt, she evaded his purpose and took shelter in a high-backed, upholstered chair with winged sides. The Louis XV chair faced away from the betraying light of the long window. *"Per favore, signore.* If we are to continue, you must respect my wishes."

Maxim followed and stood before her, leaning his arm on the fireplace mantel. "I daresay you expect me to help maintain your ruse."

"No, I merely ask that you not betray me."

"Merely ask? Do you know what you are requiring of me? From all appearances, you're an adventuress. God only knows of the chicanery you and the rest are about."

Kate looked down at her hands clenched in her lap. She was burdening him with more than an honest, upright gentleman could be expected to shoulder. What right did she have to request such a consideration? "Forgive me, Sir Maxim. I presume too far." There was a note of sad regret in her voice.

"Don't be foolish," he said softly. "Of course I'll not give you away. But I warn you the price for my silence may be far more than you bargained for. Shall we agree that I hold your unwritten note and, at a convenient time, I shall collect the debt you owe me?"

She frowned and paused before replying. "This has the makings of a very bad bargain. I daresay I'll get scorched." She glanced over at Anthony, who seemed to slumber in his chair. "Naturally, I am not without protectors, who would not view my ruination kindly.

Whatever price you exact, the business betwixt you and me must be conducted as between a lady and a gentleman. If this is agreeable to you, then we have a pact.'' She smiled. "Papa will be pleased."

"Papa? Is Mr. McClintock a relation of yours?"

She felt his probing gaze, but she would not answer him.

"He spoke of a daughter named Katherina. Is that your first name?"

For a moment, Kate sat speechless from surprise. What sort of foolishness was her father engaged in to give away her name? Then, with the composure of any great lady of the stage, she shrugged and fanned herself slowly, rhythmically.

"With your permission, I shall call you Katherina when we chance to be alone. We both know that you are not the Contessa, so it seems ludicrous to continue in that vein."

"You may address me as Miss Smith if you wish. It matters not."

"It doesn't suit you. The fan and black draping leads the mind to think beyond the commonplace. No, I shall call you Katherina." He looked intently at her. "But you aren't a shrew, are you?"

Kate laughed softly, then, leaning back into the shadows of her chair, she smiled as she plied her fan. In the momentary stillness an indistinguishable sound came from behind her and caught her attention. It was followed by the rattle of a pane of glass being pushed.

"Max," Lucy said, coming in through the long window, "how glad I am to have found you alone. I've given the slip to Mrs. Colley. She's had me closeted all morning with her, telling me how happy I'd be if I'd marry the Squire. It has been a true test of my resolve. You know how I dislike saying anything unkind about others, but, I ask you, who would want to wed the Squire? He is much too rough for my taste. And the way he chases after the Contessa has become quite disgraceful—and the way she encourages him indecent. I recommend you drop the subject of your study."

Kate leaned from behind her high-backed chair and glanced over her shoulder at the younger lady.

"Oh dear!" Lucy's entire face turned crimson. "How mortifying! Pray forgive me, Contessa. I'm sure your morals are just what they should be. I mean, no doubt they are above others of your sort." She made a helpless gesture to her brother. "Well, you know what people are bound to think when a woman travels with a retinue of handsome men. Her bodyguard is quite pleasing of person. No one can wonder at—"

"Thank you," Anthony clearly murmured from his corner.

Gasping, Lucy stared in his direction. "Oh dear!" She clamped a hand over her mouth.

"Luce, it serves you right," Maxim observed. "I see that you have some way to go before you learn to look about you more. If you'd cultivate a keener awareness you'd find yourself in fewer awkward situations."

"If—" Lucy stamped her foot at her brother "—you mean to rail at me again about my marriage to poor, unfortunate James, I shall become quite miffed with you." She addressed the room at large. "After all, isn't a lady entitled to make one mistake when she's young?"

"At least one," Kate interjected.

"How kind of you to be so understanding, Contessa." Lucy sighed and looked downcast. "Which just shows that Max was right again. I am always rushing to false conclusions. And once I find myself in a pickle I've a dreadful time extracting myself." She caught her trembling lip between her teeth before proceeding. "I originally came to visit Ivel Manor for only two weeks. I've been here nearly five months. My late husband was very attached to his aunt, you see, and I felt it behooved me to come. And then..."

"There now, Luce." Sir Maxim strode over and put an arm about his sister. "I daresay you would have found a way to leave by yourself. It was providential that your entreaty should come just when I was missing you the most."

"You missed me, Max?" Lucy sniffed and wiped the corner of her eye. "But how could you, with Mother and the rest of the family coming and going from Chiltern Hall? I know of no one else who has more guests to visit than you. People seem to like to be in your company."

Kate turned in her seat and leaned forward. The conversation interested her more with the passing of each minute. She noticed that Anthony also shared her interest, for he had left his place in the corner to draw nearer.

"Since most everyone has left the countryside for the Season in Town the Hall has been quite empty,"

Sir Maxim said. "Besides, no one oversees the servants as well as you. Now, no more nonsense. You will give the Contessa a very wrong impression of you." He turned to gaze upon Kate. A touch of devilry began to shine in his eyes. "Luce, the Contessa came to Bedfordshire for a bit of peace and to enjoy the air. Since you are familiar with the country hereabouts, why don't you take her on a tour? I daresay you would enjoy each other's company."

Kate saw through his ploy. Evidently he thought the ingenuous Lucy could discover some bits of personal information from a few leisurely hours spent together. "What a delightful plan," Kate remarked. "But I must regretfully decline. I've promised to watch the teams practice for the match."

"You are such a clever lady, madam," Maxim said, "That you would have no trouble doing both. Besides, Lucy would be utterly crushed should you refuse."

Lucy looked confused, as if not quite understanding why her brother would want her to befriend a courtesan. Then her face brightened in a smile. "What a happy notion! If you would accompany me, Contessa, then I wouldn't be required to dance attendance upon Mrs. Colley, who does so like to talk about her son. I've been here quite long enough for her to have run out of other topics. Now, it's 'Jethro says this—' or 'Jethro thinks that—' until I've begun to quote the Squire, too. And, truly, I wouldn't mind at all driving out with a lady of infamous renown. Indeed 'twould be quite exciting."

Anthony cleared his throat, catching Kate's attention. He gave her a look that said she'd better do it or else.

But Kate didn't need his prompting to decide her in favour of accompanying Lucy. A constant dose of male company had cured her of any desire to be a belle of the first order. Female companionship would be delightful. "You're quite right, Signora Gillingham, it is a happy notion. Should we find that we've run out of conversation, we can always talk about your brother. You must tell me all about him. And I will tell you all about my brothers."

"Do you have brothers, Contessa?" Lucy asked.

"Si, signora," Kate replied, giving Anthony a mischievous glance. "They can be the very devil." She turned her teasing look upon Sir Maxim, who returned it in kind. She realized that the cricket match between Biggleswade and Ickwell Green wouldn't be the only competition taking place which would require skill and ingenuity.

CHAPTER SIX

"IT IS MY OPINION," the Squire declared in a loud voice, as his team grouped together on the large expanse of lawn behind his house, "that there will be no competition. Those milksops from Ickwell will be left crying for their mothers." His blustering talk was not only intended for those huddled around him, but for the large number of gentry who'd come to observe the cricket practice.

One of the team members scratched his head as he shook it dubiously. "Ain't meanin' a disrespect, Squire. But word is goin' round that Sir Maxim's found hisself a right fine bowler with 'a hellish delivery.' Seems Sir Maxim has been workin' with the fellow these last few days."

"What!" The Squire looked incredulous. "Why haven't I heard of this player? Well, we'll just see what it takes to get him to change sides." He thought for a moment. Then, casting a glance over his shoulder at the spectators, he lowered his voice to say, "I could move the Browns out of their cottage and offer it to the fellow. The rent would be taken care of by a grateful patron."

A mutinous murmur broke out among the Biggleswade team. They appeared to want equal compensation.

The Squire puffed out his chest and glared at them. "You'll find me generous to all—a crown for any man who scores over ten points himself." The murmur grew to a rumble. "Very well, I'll cut the rents by half for any on the team who are my tenants and for the rest of you I'll pay an equal amount. But only if you beat them...and beat them soundly." The Squire strutted before his men. "The meddlesome Sir Maxim will be taught a lesson, one that will show him I'm his superior in every way."

A field-worker who stood at the back of the group snickered.

Squire Colley swung about and faced his team. "Who did that? Who dared to laugh at me?" When no one admitted to the offense, he asked, "Is this how my generosity is to be rewarded?"

His second in command stepped forward and, bowing, pulled on his forelock. "Pardon, Squire, but ye see they've heard the talk about the Contessa and Sir Maxim."

"What talk?" the Squire demanded, pulling the servile fellow away from the body of the men. "Explain yourself!"

The man hemmed and hawed before answering. "Ah— Well, Squire—" He rubbed his hands on his smock of linen drill. "We understood that the lady was claimed by you, sir. Now, what with her visitin' Sir Maxim every day at his team's practice and him walkin' out with her, the word has spread that he has cut you out of your interests—so they say."

The Squire was not amused. "But the Contessa is here first thing every morning," he said. "Don't the men *see* how she lavishes me with her attention?"

"Seems she don't stay very long. She and the Widow Gillingham have been seen driving about with that bodyguard fellow. And every day since Ickwell began their practices, the three of them join Sir Maxim for the midday meal. They eat under the trees at the edge of the green, sittin' on cushions." The fellow's tone of voice implied there was more than just eating taking place at these feasts. "Meanin' no disrespect, Squire, but are you goin' t' let some outsider steal away your mistress?"

The Squire didn't bother to correct the man's error. He enjoyed having everyone believe that the Contessa was his. Now, making a robustious show, like a bull denied his rites of spring, the Squire charged off towards his stables, saying, "Let no man stand in my way! I'll not take this insult! Today, there will be blood!"

This bold pronouncement set the onlookers to twittering. Those local gossips who'd been privileged to hear it could hardly wait to spread the word and hastened to their conveyances.

After a few minutes the Squire gratified the wishes of his team members and those still standing about by riding out of the stable yard at a blistering pace. They cheered and ran after him. There was nothing quite so fine as a fight to while away the afternoon doldrums.

KATE SAT BACK LAZILY against the trunk of a tree and gazed upward at an intrepid fellow painting the striped maypole, which stood in the middle of the green. His hazardous task seemed at odds with the tranquillity of the village. For here halcyon trees nobly sheltered the smith and the low-eaved, thatched cottages, imparting a cozy aspect to the scene.

The idyllic setting was only slightly marred by the vigorous activity of the men assembled on a portion of the immense village green. They were engaged in a drill of sorts, one designed to perfect their batting skills. The Ickwell Green team seemed intent upon an eventual victory. And, with equal fervour, they put forth their best efforts to please their new patron and captain.

During Ickwell's first days of practice, Kate had seen how Sir Maxim had gradually won the respect of his team. He'd eased into his position of command, offering a word of advice at just the right moment, giving approval when merited, and withholding any words of condemnation. But it was his insight which really engendered their respect. He knew that most of the team members were working men—farmers, shopkeepers and even a blacksmith. As such, the men had to find the time for practice and, understanding the press of their duties, Sir Maxim made sure that the hour or two he took out of their day was used profitably.

Kate was gratified to see that her reading of his character had not been far from the truth. As she observed him now a short distance away, strolling with Lucy, she had to smile. He was questing again. She wondered what sort of information he was trying to extract from his sister, for they were deep in conversation. His head bent down as if he wished to catch every word Lucy said.

Plucking a blade of springtime grass and feathering it back and forth over her chin, Kate almost chuckled aloud. She found it absurdly simple to divine the subject of their exchange. Lucy kept looking guiltily back in her direction and blushed every time Kate waved at her. What information Sir Maxim hoped to gain from his sister was a speculative issue, since Kate had only spoken in general terms to Lucy of her life and family.

Lucy, however, had bubbled forth with anecdotes and childhood reminiscences about her kith and kin. Her brother, Max, was her favourite topic. She seemed to think he was the finest gentleman in the land, and that not even Wellington could come up to his mark.

Kate knew she could make no such comparison, as she had never met the nation's hero. But, by far, Maxim was indeed the finest gentleman of her acquaintance. She'd come to admire his pleasing qualities during their walks after their alfresco luncheons. She looked forward now to their conversations. When *had* she stopped being afraid that he would betray her deception to the others? How odd to be upon cordial terms with one she ought to consider her foe.

Slowly, and with maidenly hesitancy, she began to wonder what it meant to have continual dreams about a man. Sir Maxim's image seemed to stay with her night and day.

Even now, just thinking of him made Kate uncommonly aware of her feelings and desires and she resolved to do something about it. Her eyes widened with surprise as she realized how badly she wanted to capture his deep regard. Yet, she hoped she wouldn't appear brazen in her attempt to do so. Forward ladies were such brash creatures; however, at five-and-twenty, Kate couldn't risk being demure and distant.

But, as a dowerless young woman, did she have the right to engage the interest of an eligible gentleman?

Puzzling over the dilemma, she began to drift with her thoughts and she closed her eyes to envision her dreams. A soft footfall sounded behind her, but she was unaware of anyone approaching.

"Katherina," Henry McClintock whispered, touching her shoulder. "Wake up, child. Now is not the time for sleep."

She stretched slowly, reluctant to leave her daydreams. "Papa?" She looked up into the sunlight and saw her father standing next to Anthony. "I am surprised to see you here. These last days we've sorely missed your presence."

"A man must be about his business, daughter. This venture requires my full attention, every detail must be overseen by me. Now, compose yourself and resume your role." Henry helped her to her feet.

"Very well, Papa." She assumed a proud stance. "Is this more like the Contessa? It is most difficult always to remember to be someone else. And it is exceedingly difficult when someone, who is to help, hinders one." Taking her father's proffered arm, she looked at him in puzzlement. "I must say I had not supposed *you* to be a dunderhead." Kate strolled along the edge of the village green with her father and Anthony.

Henry's offended look was eloquent.

"Yes, a dunderhead," she stated. "What other explanation is there for disclosing my Christian name to Sir Maxim?" She was not angry, merely curious.

"My dear Katherina," Henry said, "an experienced gamester must be aware of all suits if he is to take the trick." He waved his hand in a grand manner. "You say Sir Maxim knows your name. Since he has chosen to make you and your disguise the prime subject of his interest, it is only fair that we distract him with a little of the truth now and then. It will keep his mind busy." He patted Kate on the cheek. "And you shall see that he doesn't become bored. Now, I ask you, what could be more simple?"

Kate paused to appreciate her father's flare for juggling words. No matter what he said it always sounded quite reasonable. Trying to call him to account was nearly impossible as he had the talent of sidestepping any issue he wished to avoid.

She turned to Anthony. "And do you support him in this notion?"

"I don't see any way of avoiding it, do you?" Anthony asked. "Besides, what harm can come from a little light flirtation with such an agreeable gentleman? You do find him agreeable, do you not, Kate?"

"Perhaps I do. Sir Maxim is especially pleasing after time spent in the company of the Contessa's admirers, particularly the Squire."

Just behind her back, her father and brother shared a look. The elder McClintock winked at his son, who grinned in return.

Kate caught Anthony's expression. "What are you two hatching? 'Something is rotten in the state of Denmark,'" she said with a dramatic touch.

"My dear," said Henry in a remonstrative voice, "one should not quote Shakespeare so early in the day. It fevers the mind." He waved his hand airily. "Hamlet is best when presented on the boards or savoured with wine by an evening fire."

"Papa, you've diverted us from the issue again." She tapped his arm with her fan. "You needn't bother to dissemble. I can see quite plainly that you and Tony are scheming. But let me warn you, do not trifle in my affairs."

Henry looked positively aghast. "You offend my fine sensibilities, daughter. I am no trifler. I am a man with a grand design, an architect of destiny."

Laughing more to herself than aloud, Kate replied, "You are an out and outer, sir." She smoothed his sleeve with her gloved hand, then patted his arm. "Your machinations inspire awe. Of late, I find myself trembling at the thought of them."

"Nervous qualms?" Anthony asked in a teasing tone. "Or are you all aflutter with the first pangs of love?"

Kate hardly slackened her pace as she strolled on, but her breath caught for a moment. She felt exposed, as if all the world were staring at her. To even utter a word about her partiality seemed to her a jinx.

It was folly to speak of love when a lady was not certain her finer feelings were returned in kind.

Assuming an imperious tone, she asked, "Tony, do you call me to book for my acting? If I appear enamoured of the Squire, believe me, it is merely the part I play."

At her words, Anthony raised his brows. "What a surprising discovery! A marvellous performance, my dear Kate. There is more of our sire in you than I've given you credit for, heretofore. You must be proud, Papa."

"That I am," said Henry. "But enough, children. Here come Sir Maxim and his sister." He waved cordially at the approaching couple.

The two parties met midway on the far side of the green and one group was formed, heading in the same direction. By some sleight of hand, Kate found herself escorted by Sir Maxim. She wondered if this manoeuvre was to be credited to Tony or to her present companion. Her suspicions tipped to favour the latter as he managed to drop back further and further from the three before them.

"A very pleasant day, is it not, Katherina?" Sir Maxim asked, his tone softening when he said her name. "Made more pleasant when one shares it with another. Such a day pulls at the heartstrings." He smiled at her roguishly.

"It was a lover and his lass,
With a hey, and a ho, and a hey nonino,
That o'er the green corn-field did pass,
In the spring time, the only pretty ring time,

When birds do sing, hey ding a ding, ding;
Sweet lovers love the spring."

"One shouldn't quote Shakespeare too early in the day lest he risk a fevered brain...or so I am told." She glanced suspiciously at him, wondering at his carefree air. Though she longed for a closer attachment to him, she would not tolerate being taken for a lightskirt. "I had not suspected that you were the sort given to making pretty speeches. You enjoy indulging in flirtation, do you, *signore*?"

Sir Maxim drew her to a halt, looking at her with frowning consideration. "The intonation of your voice leaves me in little doubt that your words were intended as a slight. Have I done you an injury? I thought we were on better terms than this."

"As did I! Of late you've been such an agreeable companion. I have enjoyed our walks together and felt sure you were a friend. Must you insult me with trifling flirtation?"

"I meant no insult. But you're a dashed fetching creature, so it's not to be wondered at if I lose my senses on such a day as this. Besides, if you considered me a true friend you'd confide in me." He initiated their promenade again.

She glanced at him shrewdly. "Could it be that Lucy failed to satisfy your curiosity today?"

"Demme! Are you part Gypsy?" His question held a hint of genuine wonder. "Your dark hair leads the mind to think of the exotic."

"Tut-tut, Sir Maxim, you misthink the matter. My ancestors came from north of the Border." If her father wished a grain of truth to be dropped now and then, she would oblige him.

He appeared taken aback. "An honest answer?"

"Of course," she replied affably. "Did you suppose I would be untruthful?"

"However did I come to be so presumptive? You have been forthright to a fault. Have you not, Contessa?"

"Katherina, if you please."

"Then Katherina is your real name?"

She inclined her head graciously and peeped at him through the veil. "Only if it pleases you. 'And be it moon, or sun, or what you please: and if you please to call it a rush-candle, henceforth I vow it shall be so for me.'"

"La! but I am dumbfounded by your accommodating disposition. It leaves my mind in a whirl." There was a decided twinkle of amusement in his eyes.

"Brain fever," she concluded decisively. "It's the Shakespeare, don't you know?"

Chuckling, he drew her closer to his side and slowed their pace to that of a snail. "I've a premonition that furthering our acquaintance will be one of the delights of my life, but also one of its greatest challenges. You've an enigmatic air about you that is quite fascinating."

Inwardly she winced. Was her only appeal due to an aura of mystery? Did she possess nothing else that held his interest? She began to wonder and worry. Then she became impatient with herself. She knew that worrying was an empty occupation which justly merited a miser's reward.

Outwardly she kept her countenance from displaying her thoughts, and said cheerfully, "How odd that you should believe in premonitions. I'd concluded that you were the scientific sort—an academic inquisitor. A happy mistake, is it not? Men who must have facts and evidence before they can draw a conclusion are dreadfully dull." There was a teasing lilt in her voice. "I doubt they have adventures."

He remained quiet for the space of several steps, then stopped altogether. "You needn't tweak my nose, Katherina. Even my closest friends think me an eccentric." He laughed softly to himself. "I have an interest in many subjects, but lack a full knowledge of most. Therefore, I look for answers. My quest for the truth brings with it an adventure of sorts, but not the kind found in a Minerva novel."

She wondered how he knew of her fondness for novels. "That, sir, must be a backhanded way of saying I am a romantic."

"Naturally I would not wish to characterize anyone without a thorough knowledge of the person." His playful demeanour turned serious. "However are we to know each other when we continue with these children's games? It's blind man's buff with us, *cara mia.*" He took her hand in his and raised it to his lips.

"Unhand that woman!" Across the green, Squire Colley bellowed as he leaped from his horse. "Stand aside, I say! Let no man interfere."

The cricket players on the green halted their drill and gaped at him. As the Squire advanced upon the couple, the Ickwell team fell in behind him and followed. Soon Kate and Sir Maxim were surrounded by a throng of interested persons.

The Squire stood huffing and puffing. His chest expanded and contracted at an alarming rate. ''How dare you, *Sir* Maxim!'' The derisive tone of his voice caused a flutter among the bystanders. In a grandiose manner, he tugged his riding glove off and tossed it at Sir Maxim's feet. ''Consider yourself challenged!''

CHAPTER SEVEN

As THE TWO MEN STOOD facing each other, with the glove lying on the ground between them, Kate stepped into the breach.

"Scusatami," she said, assuming her role as the Contessa, "Signore Colley and Signore Maxim, this is not good." It astonished her to realize that they were fighting over her—a spinster. She tried to keep the amazement from her voice. "A public brawl is not at all the thing for gentlemen to engage in."

"You don't need to worry about me, my sweet," the Squire said, wrapping an arm possessively about her shoulders and squeezing her to him.

"Let her go." Though spoken barely above a whisper, Sir Maxim's words carried a menace.

Kate slipped out of the Squire's hold. "I will not stay if you continue to act so boorishly." She turned from them, flicking the train of her gown impatiently behind her. With a regal lift of her chin, she said, "True gentlemen have never quarrelled in my presence."

"We can settle this matter another time," said the Squire, looking quite confident. "After our Seconds have agreed upon a suitable day and place."

"Che cretino!" Kate swung around and glared at the Squire. "Do you not hear me when I speak? No man will die in a duel because of the Contessa D'Alessandria." She struck a tragic pose. "I still grieve over the loss of a most particular friend. He fought a duel for me. They brought his body to me afterward. His face was whitened by death, but his coat was reddened by his blood."

The Squire swaggered up to her and bowed. "Never knew you cared quite so much for me, my sweet. Your devotion shall be rewarded. I'll make you my Lady of the May." He pinched her cheek. "But your fears for my safety are wasted. No man has ever dared to face me on the field of honour." Glancing disdainfully at Sir Maxim, he said loudly, "The world is filled with cowards."

The glint in Maxim's eyes became more fixed. The mulish set of his jaw attested to his resoluteness.

Looking about for help, Kate saw Anthony pushing his way toward her through the crowd. But he was overtaken by an unruly mob, chanting for the Squire, and behind them came a procession of carriages and gigs from Biggleswade.

Soon the centre of the green filled with spectators, all wondering what had taken place and waiting to see what would happen next. The Ickwell team, led by Bellamy Rowden, and their supporters jostled to take their place behind Sir Maxim. In short order, most of the men had chosen which man they wished to side with.

Bellamy Rowden nudged his way forward to join the principal contenders. "Well, Squire," he said in a jocular tone, "I daresay your mother doesn't know about this sorry pass. 'Tis the sort of tomfoolery she would not appreciate." His demeanour turned to one of mocking piety. "Let me remind you of the words from the Book of Common Prayer—'Why is thy wrath against the sheep of thy pasture? How long wilt thou be angry? Shall thy jealousy burn like fire for ever?' "

"Just what is your meaning, devil-catcher?" The Squire pushed his broad chest into Bellamy's. Being taller than the would-be rector, Squire Colley managed to bury the fellow's face in his waistcoat. "And what the deuce are you doing here, anyway? Shouldn't you be out running down old folks with your gig?"

Bellamy Rowden's reply was muffled until he stepped back from the Squire's chest. "As I was saying, I've found a much more diverting pastime. I'm the prime bowler for the Ickwell team." He grinned in impish delight.

"What!" The Squire's chest swelled beyond any measure he'd heretofore achieved. The top buttons of his waistcoat popped off, pelting Mr. Rowden. "This is an outrage! I know who's behind this—this conspiracy." He swung about to face Sir Maxim. "It's you! Now, answer my challenge, or be branded a coward, sir!"

Calmly watching the blusterer before him, Sir Maxim replied in a quiet voice, "I am a guest in your house. I would not repay your mother's kindness by putting a hole in her son. There are rules about such things."

"Coward!" The Squire spat out the word.

Sir Maxim stood his ground. Not even by so much as a twitch did he indicate that he had heard the insult, but though his face remained passive, his blue eyes darkened.

At the fringe of the crowd shoving matches started between the opposing teams, leading to a great deal of noise and confusion. A chaotic swirl began to build around the two combatants.

"Signori," Kate said, rapping them both on the arms with her fan, "I will leave—leave this very day, this very hour—if you do not cease your quarrel. Please recall that I came to the country to escape this sort of nonsense." She held out her hands, calling attention to her carriage dress of Spanish blue. "I will not again wear black. There must be no duel." She looked about her. "And bring your men to order this very minute. *Sbrigati!*"

"What?" The Squire appeared taken aback.

"She said to be quick about it," explained Sir Maxim. Yet he waited for the Squire to make the first conciliatory move.

Bellamy Rowden stepped between them. "Gentlemen, I suggest you do as she requests before we have two battered teams unfit for the match. 'To every thing there is a season, and a time.' This is hardly the time. Shall you agree to cry truce?"

The two seemed unwilling to make amends, and Kate could see that each possessed a degree of stubbornness that would not easily be overridden. Railing at them failed, so she decided to use more persuasive measures.

"Squire," she called in a husky voice. He immediately came to her. She caressed the lapels of his coat and pursed her lips into a pout. Taking his arm, she led him a little way from Sir Maxim. "You are making me *molta* unhappy. Do you wish for me to be unhappy, *signore*?"

"No, of course not. But—"

"You are so strong." She ran her hand over his arm. "No one dare doubt your manliness. Yet, even though you are big and have much vigour, I know you are not cruel. I cannot bear a man who is hard in his heart." Repressing her innate modesty, she trailed her finger over his waistcoat and made heart-shaped patterns on his chest. "I would consider it a great favour, *signore,* if you would agree to withdraw your challenge."

"Well—"

"Perhaps some day I can return a favour to you." Her tongue played over her lips.

He groaned and began to breathe heavily.

"Patience, *caro mio.* I have not yet completed my mourning. It would be a sin to come to you too soon." Kate swallowed, pushing down the repugnance that surged within her. "I will give you my handkerchief—like a lady's colours—to wear during the, ah, grasshopper—or do you call it a cricket—game? No matter. You must wear my token over your heart." Coyly, she proffered her hand to him and let him fawn over it. Then she drifted from him and glided over to Sir Maxim.

"Here's a sweet quandary," Maxim murmured. "I don't know who I'd like to strangle more—our corset-busting Squire or you, my dear."

She shrugged and smiled. "One of us must be conciliating."

"Conciliating! Demme, I call that out-and-out seduction."

"You could reform me."

He looked at her with a wicked glance. "Perhaps I could. It would prove interesting to try. Your warm nature is deserving of one who would not misuse you. Katherina," he whispered, "I want..."

She waited for him to finish but he seemed to wrestle with his thoughts. "You want? Ah, you are desirous of making peace with the Squire. An excellent notion."

"A very stupid notion."

"But the most logical one." She touched his arm in a gesture of entreaty. "If you take his challenge, as a gentleman, you will be required to leave Ivel Manor. I should miss you." She paused, overwhelmed by realizing how much she would miss him. "And if you did meet the Squire at dawn he might place a lucky shot and kill you, or *you* might have to flee the country." With hand on hip, she stated, "This nonsense is not worthy of you. He's a fool and you know it. As a man of thought...and action, you must recognize that this will not do."

"Where the deuce did you learn to wheedle in such convincing style?"

"My father is a man of many talents, as are you. Cease attempting to divert the issue. Reconcile...if only because I ask it of you." She placed her hand on his for a moment and smiled at him in quite the most special manner.

Sir Maxim bowed to her. Then, turning to address the Squire and those about him, he said, "Let this matter be settled on the field—the cricket field. Squire, we meet in a fortnight. If it pleases you, we shall then resolve what is between us. May the best team win!"

DURING THE NEXT FORTNIGHT, Kate divided her time equally between the two teams and their captains. Her moments alone with Sir Maxim became fewer and fewer as interest in viewing the practices grew. It wasn't long before her enthusiastic group of admirers began to move with her from place to place. Some were recruited to join the teams. Soon the gentry and the labourers were joined in a common cause. The honour of the village and the larger town had to be defended. And no better opportunity arose to prove one's dashing manliness to the Contessa.

Indeed everyone seemed satisfied with the turn of events. Henry McClintock's winnings were growing weekly. The townsfolk and the gossips had much to occupy them. Each team went about with a greater sense of purpose.

Only three individuals were dissatisfied. The Squire's randy appetites longed to be satisfied by the Contessa. Kate had the dickens of a time keeping the man at a safe distance. And Sir Maxim simmered from watching the lout make advances upon Katherina.

In the evenings the atmosphere at Ivel Manor grew decidedly strained, but Mrs. Colley kept everyone so busy with social engagements that there was no time for quarrelling. Although attending the practices had become a pastime for the local gentry, it was the card parties, the small assemblies and routs they relished most. At these functions they could stay abreast of the gossip and see how the competition fared between the Squire and Sir Maxim.

Kate found that by encasing herself with her admirers each evening neither team captain could gain the advantage over the other as far as the Contessa was concerned. Though she longed for Sir Maxim's company, she resolutely denied herself that privilege. Fear of what might occur kept her aloof and circumspect in both her flirtations.

She counted the days until at last the great day of the match dawned. Lingering clouds from the gentle showers the night before drifted slowly southward, and the sun cast its warmth over the countryside, beckoning all to sally forth.

Not only did the residents of Ickwell and Biggleswade turn out in full force, but many others from the surrounding communities as well. The roads to Biggleswade become choked with all manner of hacks, carts and carriages. Their destination was the large, seven-acre meadow located just beyond the town which the Squire had bought and turned into a cricket ground.

Ensconced in one of the Squire's carriages, Kate sat vis-à-vis Anthony and Polonius. She glanced down at the side panel of the conveyance. "Is there nothing *he* has not set his name to? I feel like a branded woman."

"As the Colonel is wont to say," remarked Polonius, "'I ain't seen a *JGC* on the Contessa, not yet,'" His inflection was the perfect mimic of the Colonel's.

"Do you feel owned, Kate?" asked Anthony.

"I feel I am on display," she replied. "I ride in the Squire's landau, I shade myself with a gift from the Squire—" she twirled the parasol she held aloft "—and I am to sit in the Squire's specially erected pavilion. He wants everyone to think he owns me. If he doesn't figure some way to put a *JGC* on me by week's end I'll be surprised."

"You must not have taken note of the design," Anthony said, pointing to the pagoda-shaped shade. The leaves painted on the cloth formed a series of *JGC*s.

Kate snapped the parasol shut. "He thinks to claim me with a trifle. The Squire has no sense of value. I am almost of a mind to teach him the worth of a woman's virtue."

"Is that the price in Mayfair or Covent Garden?" Polonius asked, with the brashness of a young man. "A woman's virtue can be had for a pittance in certain parts of Town."

"Which only shows," Kate said, "how little some men regard females and how some females regard themselves." The strength behind her words caught her brothers' attention.

"Didn't mean a disrespect," Polonius muttered.

"Have you thought of what's to become of me if Papa does not succeed?" she asked. "I left my last situation so abruptly that Mrs. Bagworth can hardly be faulted for not giving me a character. Without a recommendation, how am I to secure employment as a companion? If I cannot gain honest employment, what is left to me? Shall I become Covent Garden ware? Will my virtue be bought for a few pence?"

Polonius regarded her as if struck on the face.

Sliding forward, Anthony clasped her hands in his. "Don't lose heart, my dear. Papa will come through." He grinned. "Yet if the unforeseeable occurs, I shall take care of you. We may be down, Kate, but we're not finished. Come! Where's that ready smile? This is hardly the day for the blue devils."

She squared her shoulders and chased away her doldrums with a smile. "I hope Sir Maxim beats the breeches off the Squire's 'Biggleswade boys.'"

Though many of the public hoped the same, there were few who would back their wishes with a sizeable bet. But interest in the match ran even higher among the gamesters. Henry McClintock divided his attention between overseeing the Contessa's welfare and tending to his betting book.

Since the Squire's team was known for its excellence, not many were willing to bet against them. But Colonel Buffard and Henry McClintock made numerous wagers on Ickwell, at handsome odds. Word went out that they favoured the predicted losers and, with a little of their blunt going here or there, they bet all they had allotted for this collusion.

The cricket match was just to last the day—unlike some, which continued for two or three—ending at the setting of the sun or the completion of two innings. The spectators, who'd come prepared with provisions for the midday meal, vied for places around the outer perimeter of the ground. Those who'd been invited by the Squire to shelter under the brightly coloured pavilion happily took their places on parlour chairs and sofas which were set on soft carpets.

Making a grand entrance, the Squire's party—consisting of his mother, Lucy Gillingham, the Contessa and her minions—arrived after their guests. Mrs. Colley waved at the waiting crowd of spectators. They returned the kindness with cheers and shouts of greetings.

"I daresay, Contessa," Mrs. Colley remarked to Kate as they made their way through the assembled guests, "that we are the envy of the county. La! Who else can boast of such splendid accommodations to view a cricket match?" She swung her bell-shaped body onto a chair. "Not that I truly watch the game, but one does like to be seen at events of importance. The repast is what I enjoy the most, and my son has spared no expense to provide us with a luncheon fit for the Regent."

"The Squire is a generous host," Kate murmured. "*Certamente*, I am grateful for all his kindnesses." She saw a parasol with a similar design to hers bob above the crowd and she glared at the one she held in front of her.

Mrs. Colley glanced at it. "How charming, but you must see Lucy's. Its quality is above all others." She called the young lady to her side. "Child, let me see your parasol."

Sitting down by Mrs. Colley, Lucy looked puzzled as she held it out for inspection.

"Only see how the leaves form such a delightfully clever design—*JGC*s." Mrs. Colley pointed the pattern out to Kate. "My son likes to give these little gifts to those for whom he feels a significant affinity." She patted Lucy on the knee. "There now, you mustn't blush over the attention he shows you. I am sure the special notice he pays is only your due."

Kate eased her parasol behind her, intent upon getting rid of the thing before anyone took note of it. Did the Squire buy his tokens of affection in bulk, she wondered, thus getting a reduced price?

"Here, Contessa," Mrs. Colley said, motioning to her, "you must take this seat next to me."

With the parasol hidden in the folds of her gown, Kate eased onto the parlour chair. While making a pretense of spreading her skirts, she lowered the offending object onto the carpet and shoved it beneath her chair with her foot. She glanced back at her brothers, who sat just behind her, and noted their amused expressions.

"Lucy," their hostess said, "draw your chair closer to mine. You know, dear girl, how I depend on you to be near me. The Squire says it is your accommodating nature that makes you such an agreeable companion."

Lucy looked like a worried hedgehog who wished to hide in a hole in the ground. "Maxim says that I am much too stubborn, like him, to be wholly agreeable. But my mother will be gratified to know that her strictures have made me acceptable company. Since I'd married so young, she was fearful that I would not know how to go in the world."

"And such a splendid bride you were for my dear nephew, God rest his soul," said Mrs. Colley, "and you will yet make a splendid bride for another. Jethro often says that he yearns for just such a bride as his cousin was blessed with. There's no law against marrying your cousin's widow.''

"More's the pity," mumbled Lucy into her clutched handkerchief.

Kate leaned over her hostess and offered Lucy the use of her hartshorn. "This talk of Signora Gilligham's departed husband seems to oversét her." Looking toward the field, Kate called the older woman's attention to the appearance of the Squire. "Your *figlio*, how important he looks."

From his tent which was placed at one end of the meadow, the Squire marched out before the crowd. He raised his arm in Caesar-like fashion as a recognition of the polite applause he received.

In the middle of the grounds Sir Maxim, dressed in waistcoat and breeches, and two umpires stood waiting. The Squire took his time approaching them and, upon reaching the trio, he clapped his chosen Biggleswade umpire on the back, saying, "We want a fair game, now. Here's the coin for the toss." He palmed the piece of silver to his man.

"'Tis traditional that this coin be used, Squire,'' said Ickwell's umpire, an ancient now stooped by time and the weight of being known as a sage. He held up a worn farthing. "No one is a sure winner with this coin. It has two sides."

The Squire stepped back, looking aghast, but nevertheless he took the silver coin from the Biggleswade umpire and slipped it in his pocket. Though muttering, he made no protest.

With a captain on each side of him, the old man tossed up the farthing. While it still spun in the air, Sir

Maxim called heads and, as luck would have it, won the toss.

Sir Maxim decided that his team would bat first. He lined them up in the order they were to go—putting first the two with strong defensive powers and good nerve, then the most brilliant run-getters and, lastly, the weakest of the batsmen. Eleven men, brave and true, stood divested of their coats, waiting to swing at the opposition.

The Biggleswade boys took to the field in the midst of warm applause. The Squire took his stance as the initial bowler, but before he let loose the ball he saluted those who sat in the pavilion. Pulling a bit of lace from beneath the breast of his waistcoat, he waved a handkerchief—the Contessa's token of regard.

Kate acted as if he were paying his tribute to Lucy and his mother, but the longer she waited to recognize his particular attention, the more vigorously he waved.

"Signora Colley," Kate said, "should we not give the Squire his due?"

At Mrs. Colley's instigation, the whole party in the pavilion stood and applauded. The Squire's chest filled as an extension of his pride. He strutted around and made a great business of getting ready to bowl.

Bellamy Rowden, the first batter, took his place before the wicket. He grinned at the Squire, who glared back and then turned his hard gaze upon Sir Maxim. And thus the contest began.

Kate tried to follow the match, but her knowledge of cricket was minimal. By the look of each team and the reaction of the spectators, she judged that Ickwell

Green was taking a commanding lead. She confirmed this by turning often to her brothers for an explanation.

Those in the pavilion seemed to think the cricket match a social function. Kate's view of the field was often blocked by guests who desired to mingle and gossip with the others. Nevertheless she managed to keep track of Sir Maxim. Each time he batted she witnessed the soundness of his judgement and the disciplined strength he possessed, for the Squire could not bowl him out.

As the morning advanced, Kate became increasingly aware of Sir Maxim's lean, muscular physique. So distracted did she become by his presence that she could hardly remember to behave as the Contessa.

Colonel Buffard hobbled into the pavilion and approached Kate. "Well, Contessa, what do you think of our Ickwell lads? A fine bunch, are they not?"

"I've seen none better," Kate said. Her gaze was locked upon Sir Maxim.

"Just wait until the Squire's team comes to bat," proclaimed Mrs. Colley. "Then you will be privileged to see the very best."

"I must differ with your opinion, ma'am." The Colonel leaned towards the ladies. "Sir Maxim is a man to be reckoned with. In the space of a mere three weeks, he's refined a raw bunch of bumpkins into a finely skilled body of men." He winced when one of the Ickwell team was stumped out. "Well, you cannot expect miracles, but our captain has done what none other was willing to do. And, mark my words, you will see the fruits of his labours today and be amazed.''

Watching Sir Maxim stretch before once again taking his turn as striker, Kate fanned herself, trying to cool her unladylike longings. ''*Scusi, signore,* but is it the custom for the players to go without their coats?''

''It's a commonsense necessity that they do go without.'' The Colonel gazed up at the sky. ''Should it turn warm, they'll likely play without even their waistcoats.''

The sudden vision of Sir Maxim in just shirtsleeves left Kate limp.

''Contessa,'' the Colonel exclaimed, ''are you feeling faint?''

Anthony was at her side before she could disclaim any sensation of illness. He assisted her to her feet and led her out of the pavilion to a cluster of trees.

''Kate, is something wrong?'' Anthony looked down at her in concern.

She smiled reassuringly up at him. ''I am merely being a ninnyhammer.'' She strolled under the beech trees and found a fallen log to sit on. ''Tony, why is it that the sight of a man without his coat should stir me?''

''There's a magic that occurs between the genders that is inexplicable,'' he said as he sat down beside her. ''Being a refined and restrained young lady, you have not allowed yourself to feel the compelling force that draws a man and a woman to each other. Or have you?''

''I've seen you and Polonius nearly naked and was not troubled in the least, but today...'' Kate glanced around quickly and, seeing no one, raised her veil to fan her face. She sighed heavily. "Is not affection a pure and worthy feeling? Then if one has this feeling for another how does one reason away unworthy thoughts concerning that person?"

"Unworthy?"

Kate nibbled the end of her thumb. "Thoughts of a physical nature...longings that warm the skin and flush the cheeks."

"Aha!" His voice held a note of surprised discovery. "My dear sister, as your brother, I must tell you that these inclinations for the flesh are sanctioned only after marriage. If you find a man for whom you have an affection *and* these inclinations, you are allowed to surrender to your desires *after* the vows are spoken."

"Perhaps he doesn't wish to wed me."

"Then if he touches you, I shall call the blackguard out!"

She silently stared at him for a moment, then asked, "Is kissing permissible?"

Anthony rubbed his chin, seeming to wrestle with what he should say. "Kissing often leads to dangerous territory. I am determined, Kate, that you shall not become Covent Garden ware...all from a broken heart." He brushed her cheek with his finger. "Love is the very devil, my dear."

In his voice she heard a sad poignancy. "Have you loved, Tony?"

He scoffed at himself. "How can I love honourably when I am without a fortune or a future?"

They sighed together.

CHAPTER EIGHT

TROUBLED BY THEIR OWN THOUGHTS, Kate and Anthony sat silently for a long while on the log. Then into the quiet that had settled between them, a clamorous uproar intruded. Kate exchanged a puzzled look with her brother.

"What's amiss?" she asked, getting to her feet. They hurried back to the meadow to find the answer. She stopped short at the sight before her.

In the middle of the cricket field Sir Maxim held the fallen Bellamy Rowden, who grimaced and clutched his shoulder, while a few of the Ickwell players huddled around.

Standing aloof from the group was the Squire, his arms crossed defensively over his chest. The rest of the team appeared ready to hang him from the nearest tree. A number of the spectators shook their fists, shouted boos or hissed loudly at him. Even the Squire's own team stepped back from him.

"Foul!" cried the Ickwell umpire.

The Squire's face reddened with indignation. "Balderdash! It was a freakish mishap."

"You struck the ball in just such a way so that it would hit the lad," the ancient stated. "He bowled out two of your Biggleswade boys and you wanted him stopped.''

Blustering, the Squire turned away from the Ickwell umpire and appealed to the onlookers. ''I ask you, am I the sort of man who would do such a deed? Well? I dare any man here to step forward and call me a cheat.''

These words cooled the heat of the jeerers and they grew silent. The mood of the crowd, though, did not bode well for Squire Jethro Gillingham Colley. He strutted about with his hands on his hips, as if daring any to defy him.

The elderly Ickwell umpire tapped him on the back and said, ''You'll sit out your turn, sir, and not bat until the close of the inning.''

''What!''

''Would you rather receive a penalty and forfeit the match?'' The small elderly fellow seemed not at all intimidated by the large Squire.

The Biggleswade team soothed the Squire as best they could, and though making a great show of fuming, the Squire seemed to accept the umpire's decision.

Meanwhile, after making sure that young Mr. Rowden was seen by a physician, Sir Maxim tried to calm his men. He stood at length quietly talking to them. When at last they turned and faced their opponents, they possessed an unmistakable air of sober determination. Resolutely, they took to the field again.

Sir Maxim replaced Mr. Rowden as bowler. Picking up the ball, he tossed it several times into the air as he contemplated the stumps and bail. In three consec-

GET 4 BOOKS

FREE

Return this card, and we'll send you 4 brand-new Harlequin Regency™ novels, absolutely FREE! We'll even pay the postage both ways!

We're making you this offer to introduce you to the benefits of the Harlequin Reader Service®: free home delivery of brand-new romance novels, AND at a savings of 26¢ apiece compared to the cover price!

Accepting these 4 free books places you under no obligation to continue. You may cancel at any time, even just after receiving your free shipment. If you do not cancel, every other month we'll send 4 more Harlequin Regency novels, and bill you just $2.49* apiece–that's all!

Yes, please send me my 4 free Harlequin Regency novels, as explained above.

Name

Address   Apt.

City   State   Zip

248 CIH 4AJR (U-H-RG-07/90)

DETACH ALONG DOTTED LINE AND MAIL TODAY! – DETACH ALONG DOTTED LINE AND MAIL TODAY! – DETACH ALONG DOTTED LINE AND MAIL TODAY!

Get 4 Books FREE

SEE BACK OF CARD FOR DETAILS

utive deliveries he took the wickets, which left Biggleswade with only five batters to finish the inning.

Watching his fluid movements and strength, Kate felt the need to fan herself again. Yet she was amused to notice that she wasn't the only one warmed by his exertions.

Across the field she saw the Squire pull out the handkerchief she'd given him as a token. He repeatedly dabbed his brow with it, and then began to gnaw on its lace edge as the game progressed. He looked relieved when a different bowler replaced Sir Maxim, but even so, one by one, his batters were reduced in number.

When at last the Squire was allowed to bat, he stepped before the wicket with a trepid demeanour. Some of his bravado returned when he received shouts of encouragement from the loyal Biggleswade supporters. He swung the stick a few times, each swing more powerful than the last. It was up to him to get a good hit so that his team could continue to score in the inning. He planted his feet and stood ready, then, as he gazed at the opposite wicket, his eyes widened with dismay.

Saluting in a manner similar to that of a fencer greeting his opponent, Sir Maxim grinned cordially at the Squire before picking up the ball to resume as his team's bowler. After a moment of study, he made a different sort of delivery, which startled the Squire. The ball zinged by the batter and struck down the bail.

"Foul!" cried the Squire, flinging his bat to the ground. "Round-arm bowling ain't cricket!"

"Says who?" One of the Ickwell men advanced upon him, hands balled into fists.

It started as a small dispute and grew suddenly into a thoroughgoing brawl. The Ickwell and Biggleswade teams knocked into each other like rams butting heads.

The Squire squared off with Sir Maxim, who expertly lifted his pair of fives as they circled slowly, eyeing one another. Without warning, the Squire rushed in with his mighty fist raised. Yet before he could execute his punch, Sir Maxim came at him with a flourish and laid him out with one final, powerful blow. The Squire, cross-eyed, tried to get up, but fell back in a stupor.

All around Sir Maxim the fighting raged on. Brandishing his cane, Colonel Buffard whisked by him on the shoulders of Ickwell's blacksmith. As they passed through the jostling men, the Colonel clouted any of the Biggleswade team he came across.

Even many of the spectators dashed into the fray, taking sides with their favourite team. In the midst of the hair-pulling, eye-gouging and jaw-breaking, Anthony attempted to keep Kate safe. But when he acted as her shield he became a target, and she was left with no protector.

She ran this way and that, dodging bodies and swinging elbows. While she tried to stay clear of the fracas, someone collided with her and pitched her deeper into the brawl. With a hand on her hat and an arm before her face, she bent over and pushed her way forward.

"Contessa!" Bellamy Rowden cried. He appeared quite recovered from his injury. "Ma'am, this is no place for a lady." He delivered a facer to the man he held by the shirtfront, let him crumble to the ground, and then offered his arm to Kate. "Allow me to see you to your chair in the pavilion."

One of the Contessa's admirers from Biggleswade saw her with the cleric and grabbed hold of him. "If anyone's to help the lady from the field it will be a Biggleswade man."

Kate drew back as a new quarrel broke out, and ran, quite by accident, straight into the circle of Sir Maxim's arms. Her eyes focused on the dark hair, peeping out of his open-necked shirt. "Unhand me, sir," she said in a low, husky voice.

He grasped her arm and slung her bodily over his shoulder. "Katherina, be still!" he commanded when she squirmed. He wrapped an arm around her thighs, then pushed his way out of the thick of the melee.

Carried like a rolled carpet, Kate had to place her hand on his back for balance. Through her glove and his waistcoat and shirt she felt the warmth and firmness of his body. Unladylike thoughts entered her mind.

"Sir Maxim," she called, uttering his name with difficulty. "This will not do. The gossips will make much of it."

"Let them."

A wisp of cool air tickled her leg as he strode across the expanse of grass, sidestepping or, if necessary, knocking down any who got in his way. In their wake, she saw startled faces. She began to laugh. "Truly, sir, this is most improper."

He responded by merely shifting her on his shoulder and continuing onward to the pavilion.

As they neared the edge of the field, Colonel Buffard breezed by on the back of the stalwart blacksmith. "Tally-ho!" the Colonel exclaimed, barely missing Kate's head with a swing of his cane. "There's not been a fracas like this since the match in '07. Tally-ho!" He prodded the brawny fellow beneath him. "Away, Tom!"

From her position on Maxim's shoulder, Kate saw how serious the foray was getting. If it wasn't stopped soon many men would be seriously injured. She began to consider the best means for bringing it to a halt.

But when at last Maxim set her down, her thoughts treacherously took an amorous turn. Her hands lingered on his arms as she gazed up at him. Her senses became lost in his blue eyes.

It was only the sounds of renewed fury which recalled her to her sense of purpose. She stepped back from him. "Sir Maxim, would you lend your aid to bringing order on the field? Perhaps if you rallied your Ickwell men and—"

"Contessa! Are you unharmed?" asked Mrs. Colley, as she shoved her vinaigrette under Kate's nose. "You should not have allowed Sir Maxim to handle you so. It's not at all genteel. This brawling, though, goes beyond the pale—quite dreadful, really." She darted a glance at the field. "Did you see the Squire out there?"

With eyes watering, Kate drew back from the bottle's vinegary assault. "No, but maybe Sir Maxim has."

"I believe he is lying out in the middle of it all," he said stoically.

"My poor boy!" Mrs. Colley wrung her hands. "We must help him."

"And so we shall," replied Kate. "Sir Maxim, please see to your men while Mrs. Colley and I gather the women together."

A moment later, Sir Maxim sprang up onto his carriage, startling his groom, and drove the equipage out to the middle of the field. Tossing the reins to his man, he leaped down and came away with two of his Ickwell players.

Bellamy Rowden demanded to know what the deuce he meant by interfering in a man's dispute. Sir Maxim told him he was making a cake of himself and, for that matter, the whole team resembled a gang of rough-and-tumble bumpkins—hardly the sort who were determined to win a cricket match.

This reprimand quickly brought Mr. Rowden to his senses. With his aid, Sir Maxim began to pull his Ickwell men out of the worst of it.

Meanwhile, in short order, the women got organized and rushed to stand between their menfolk. Some of the gentle sex had to use direct methods to get the attention of the brawlers. Whether by the use of a parasol cracked over the head or a dousing with a jug of water, the wives and sweethearts became victors of the field.

The aged Ickwell umpire slowly shuffled to the centre of the grass. "Before this unsportsmanlike conduct, the lawfulness of a round-arm delivery was questioned. Bein' as I'm the principal umpire of this match and havin' by far the greatest experience in such matters my word will be final. I say that since the Marylebone Cricket Club—which is the first authority in all things concernin' cricket—has not ruled against a round-arm delivery, it be permitted."

Leaning inertly against Sir Maxim's carriage, the Squire was too befuddled to make a protest. But a disgruntled murmur arose from the Biggleswade supporters.

"Since Sir Maxim's delivery was a lawful one," the Ickwell umpire continued, "the Squire is deemed bowled down. Thus the inning is over with the score standing at sixty-eight for Biggleswade and seventy-one for Ickwell Green. The second inning will begin after the teams have dressed their wounds and eaten a midday repast."

WITH THE SECOND INNING OVER, even when the sun dipped low in the sky, no one seemed intent upon leaving the cricket ground. The Biggleswade team stood about looking dumbfounded as the men of Ickwell Green threw their hats in the air and cheered. Still the supporters of the losing team could not begrudge the winners their display of jubilation.

The match had been closely played. Biggleswade had increased their runs by a handsome margin, leaving Ickwell quite a challenge when they came to bat. But with such a fine captain as Sir Maxim, the score was soon tied. The honours for making the winning runs went to Bellamy Rowden, who snatched the bail from the wicket before being hoisted up on his team-mates' shoulders. Sir Maxim was similarly honoured by others from Ickwell.

The only ones more jubilant than the winning Ickwell players and supporters were Colonel Buffard and Henry McClintock, who'd increased their purses twofold. Though none of the bets in Henry's book were of a noteworthy amount, still the accumulation of a little here and a little there tallied into quite a profit.

In the midst of the celebrating, Kate noticed her father's joviality and she sighed with relief. It did not bear thinking of how they should have gone on if he'd lost.

"Come," Lucy said, taking Kate's hand, "we must see the ceremony. You'll excuse us, won't you, Mrs. Colley?"

The older woman waved her hand and said, "Oh, yes, go along, both of you. I've the headache." She put her hand over her eyes. "Oh, the shame of it. The Squire will be the talk of the neighbourhood. We must never mention this day in his hearing. It would be cruel to tease him so."

Before Kate and Lucy could escape from the pavilion, Anthony stepped between them, offering each an arm of escort. "Ka—that is, Contessa," he said, "I insist upon accompanying you both. One never knows when..." He touched his bruised jaw and cut lip, reminders of that morning's brawl, and then locked arms with his sister. He stiffened, though, when Lucy lightly placed her hand upon his arm.

His distant but gallant behaviour towards Lucy puzzled Kate. To cover her brother's curious manner, she made inconsequential conversation as they strolled out onto the field. "What ceremony is to take place, Signora Gillingham?"

"The Squire explained it all to me," Lucy said. "But in his version Biggleswade was to be the victor and he would make a speech as he accepted the honour of retaining the Champion's Chalice. Then he was to choose the Lady of the May. He told me that I would be his choice."

"A promise he bestows like parasols," murmured Kate in an aside to her brother.

"No doubt," Anthony said softly. "Ah—no doubt Sir Maxim will confer the tribute on one who has both grace and beauty—you, Signora Gillingham." He bowed to Lucy.

The young widow blushed, but shook her head. "Brotherly fondness is a poor substitute for a certain partiality. Don't you agree?" She gazed at Anthony's profile, then looked away.

Anthony took a deep breath, but would not comment.

The strained silence lasted until they reached the presentation stand—a wooden platform that had been constructed across the field from the pavilion. A crowd had already gathered, but a passageway was made for the Contessa and Sir Maxim's sister.

The Colonel, as one of the governing officials of Ickwell Green, conducted the ceremonies. "It's with everlasting pleasure that I award to our own team this chest of prize money—two hundred guineas. Of course, the amount might not be quite as handsome as the sum which the Squire wagered with a certain party." He slapped his knee and chortled, then looked about as if missing someone. "Where *is* the Squire?"

A guard of men comprised of the Squire's Biggleswade boys conveyed their captain to the platform. They even shoved him up the steps, since his stupefaction over the loss rendered him quite inane.

"Well, Squire Jethro Gillingham Colley," the Colonel said, "it's a good thing you didn't put a *JGC* on this silver chalice...for it ain't yours, not yet." He slapped him on the back.

The Squire swayed. With the aid of two of his Biggleswade boys, he retained his footing. His glazed face might have been mistaken for that of a dead man's, so fixed was his expression.

"Friends, neighbours, ladies and gentlemen," the Colonel said in a carrying voice, "it's with the happiest of hearts—and I ain't felt this good since I visited the Widow Drury last summer—that I present the Champion's Chalice to the captain of this year's winning team. I give you," he paused importantly, "Sir Maxim Wolverton!"

The crowd broke into cheers of "huzzah!" and the fife and drum company of the local militia played a fanfare. Advancing through the backslapping throng in his shirtsleeves, braces and breeches, Sir Maxim weaved his way to the platform, pausing briefly to nod at Kate and smile at his sister. After a moment, he took his place next to the Colonel.

"Sir Maxim," said the old war-horse, "we are a grateful people. You've restored the honour of Ickwell Green." He wiped his eyes and sniffed, then held up the Champion's Chalice. "I deliver this cup into your safekeeping for the space of one year."

"Thank you, sir." Sir Maxim took it and looked at it thoughtfully. "But the Champion's Chalice belongs to the entire Ickwell team; therefore I, in turn, entrust it to the village taverner, with the request that he display it in a place of honour." This pleased the crowd greatly.

The Colonel clapped Sir Maxim on the back and raised a shout of huzzah. "It is our tradition that—" he referred to a slip of paper for the exact wording "—the winning captain assume the homage which is his due by accepting the distinction of becoming the Lord of the May. And known as such, you shall reign at Ickwell's May Day festivities along with your Lady of the May—a female of your choosing."

Sir Maxim looked out among the crowd. A flurry of female twittering answered his regard.

The Colonel rapped the boards with his cane for silence. "Ladies, maidens and unmarried females of any age, please prepare yourselves for the gentleman's perusal. The rest of you fall back." He motioned for the new Lord of the May to precede him.

With a reticent mien, Sir Maxim took the steps slowly and passed by Kate and Lucy. He didn't appear to relish his task.

"Well," Lucy said quietly, "I knew he wouldn't likely pick me, but, Contessa, to give you the go-by is most perplexing. I thought he considered you a friend . . . a particular friend."

"Some men do not acknowledge their particular friends in public, *signora*." Kate was glad that the veil and the shadows formed by the setting sun hid her expression of chagrin.

She wondered why he ignored her. She could hardly pretend to ignore him. His rolled-up sleeves revealed his strong forearms, glistening with perspiration. Gaping open to the breastbone, his shirt clung to his damp torso in a tantalizing manner. The game had demanded a state of undress that seemed to accentuate his muscularity, which had not been previously obvious in his day-to-day clothing.

Kate chastised herself for wanton thoughts. She supposed that the expression on her face—that part which could be seen—would clearly give away her wicked imaginings. She could scarcely wonder at his deeming her unworthy of recognition.

Though she tried to look away from Maxim, Kate's gaze returned again and again to him as he cut his way through the group of females. One young lady, no doubt overcome by modesty, fainted at his feet. The Colonel motioned for her parents to carry her away. Miraculously, she recovered enough to wrap her arms round one of Maxim's legs and plead that he choose her.

Sir Maxim appeared rather shocked by this display. He retreated the way he'd come. Stopping before Kate, he bowed and offered his arm.

"Would you do me the honour of becoming my Lady of the May?" he asked, and he asked it in such a way as to intimate she was the only one worthy of the title.

Though perplexed, she placed her hand lightly on his arm and walked with him up to the platform.

"You must give her a token of your regard," Bellamy Rowden shouted from the crowd.

A self-conscious smile crept over Sir Maxim's lips as he gazed at Kate. Gallantly he raised her hand. Then, regarding her with a wicked twinkle, he removed her glove and cast it at the Squire's feet. In the most intimate manner imaginable, he pressed his lips to the back of her hand.

CHAPTER NINE

ON THE FIRST DAY OF MAY, the Birchers were out making their rounds of mischief in the darkest hours of morning. They left a branch of lime on Colonel Buffard's door, which—since it rhymed with prime—was a compliment. But under the portico bearing a *JGC*, a large pile of plum branches implied the owner was glum. Before the Contessa's suite of rooms lay a sprig from a pear tree. Obviously someone thought her fair and delightsome.

Just prior to dawn a band of young gentlemen, including Bellamy Rowden and Polonius, shattered the quiet of the neighbourhood. Running from house to house, they blew tin trumpets and cow-horns.

The Squire had a thing or two to say about this untimely disturbance. He bellowed out his window at the rascals and they blew their horns back at him. After that racket no one continued to sleep.

Desirous to know if the house was on fire or what the catastrophe might be, Kate gazed sleepy-eyed out her door and found nothing amiss, only the pear-tree sprig. She felt relieved that it wasn't a stack of nuts, which meant harlot. Such a covert censure wouldn't have surprised her since the very personal way Sir

Maxim had treated her had set the gossips' tongues to wagging.

Stroking her cheek with the sprig, Kate gazed out her window, woolgathering. Soon she would don her plain cambric gown with the high neck and short train, and the pelisse of green sarsenet with the scalloped hem. She would top it all with a broad-brimmed Lavinia chip hat and, of course, the veil. Her promenade dress would make a fitting costume for the role she was about to play. For one entire day she would be Sir Maxim's lady—his Lady of the May.

She smiled to herself, remembering how outraged she had been that the Squire dared lay claim to her with his gifts and lavish treatment. Even her room, known as the Madame de Pompadour, indicated how the Squire perceived her as *his* future mistress. Its mirror-panelled walls and enormous bed were suggestive enough, but the gilded cupids went beyond subtlety. She'd been offended by the lout's presumption of ownership.

Yet she didn't at all mind being thought the lady of Maxim's choice. She revelled in the awareness that he shared the knowledge of her pretense and that he was so protective of her. Though he teased and taunted her about her role as the Contessa, still he always managed to covey that his perception of her was as a genteel woman. He was playful at times, but he never went beyond the mark.

The possibilities of furthering their friendship, especially on a day designed to celebrate the rites of spring, set her mind to speculating. Perhaps as his Lady of the May she would do some teasing of her own. Perhaps she might reveal a little more of her true self to Sir Maxim. Perhaps.

If nothing else good came from her masquerade as the Contessa, she at least would have this one day. With a heart full of anticipation, she began to dress. And as she completed her toilette, she whistled a merry tune.

SIR MAXIM HUMMED TO HIMSELF as he leaned against one of the columns which supported the portico of the Squire's residence. Even the large *JGC* chiselled overhead could not dampen his carefree mood.

In the distance he heard the frolicsome approach of the May procession. Sounds of laughter and singing grew louder and louder as the group of merrymakers neared Ivel Manor. Following behind the bearers of the May Garlands—made up of chains of cowslips and primroses twisted around light staves and joined to one large beflowered hoop—a line of young folk meandered up the gravel drive. They playfully urged on a donkey, who was pulling a dogcart fastened with brightly coloured ribbons and posies, and every now and then they stopped to caper about or joke with one another. Trailing after the revellers came the troupe of May Horns with Bellamy Rowden and Polonius.

Sir Maxim was about to greet the procession when the front doors opened and out stepped his Lady of the May. She curtsied and advanced with her hand outstretched to him. She looked quite lovely. Gone were the mourner's weeds. The only reminder of her pretense was the veil.

The only reminder, that is, until the Contessa's bodyguard followed her out.

Leading her to the side for a private word, Maxim asked, "Is he to come along with us?"

"Tony is my chaperon. He insists upon accompanying me *everywhere* I go."

Maxim motioned to the noisy procession gathering at the foot of the front steps. "Does he think I plan to ravish you before all the world? Besides, by what right does he order you about?"

"The right of a male relation," she replied glibly. "I suspect he does not trust you entirely—not since you behaved improperly that night on the terrace. You have not yet redeemed yourself in his eyes."

"Katherina, you must know that I meant you no—"

The fractious musicians with the tin trumpets and cow-horns chose that moment to raise a great noise, drowning Sir Maxim's words. The members of the procession indicated their eagerness to be on their way. They called loudly for the Lord and Lady of the May.

From an upper-storey window, the Squire thrust out his head, which was covered by a nightcap. "Quiet! Quiet, I say! Can't a man have peace in his own home? Anyone can see that I am not well." He gingerly touched his black eye. "Away! Begone! Before I send for the constable." He slammed shut the window.

Signalling that he needed a few more moments with Kate, Sir Maxim tried to quiet the merrymakers.

"It would appear that the Squire will not be attending today's festivities," Kate observed. "I believe Mrs. Colley, too, is planning to stay at home.

Your sister, Sir, will need an escort. It must be some-one who can be depended upon to safeguard a lady's reputation." Her gaze travelled over to her own chap-eron.

Sir Maxim glanced from Kate to Anthony and back again to Kate. "You can't mean— But she's my sis-ter."

"He's my brother."

"Is he, now?" Sir Maxim compared the two. "You don't look at all related."

"That may be, but there was nothing irregular about our parentage. I am said to have the features of my mother's family and Tony is the image of Papa in his younger years."

Sir Maxim's chuckle held an incredulous tone. "This is a surprising come-about. For weeks and weeks you've been as close as a clam concerning your history. What game are you playing, my dear?"

"It's a May Game, sir. Come along." In short or-der she persuaded Tony to be Lucy's escort. Then, taking Sir Maxim's arm, she descended the steps in a grand manner, as befitting a Lady of the May.

Pushed forward by the others in the procession, Bellamy Rowden acted as the spokesman. He bowed low and said, "We come as emissaries of the merry spirit which epitomises this day and adjure you, mi-lord and milady, to observe the traditions along with us. Behold your royal chariot." He waved an arm to-wards the dogcart.

Amid the cacophony of laughter and horn blow-ing, Sir Maxim helped Kate up to the forward-facing seat. He took his place facing in the opposite direction, so that they sat shoulder to shoulder.

Leading off with the May Garland, the revellers continued on their way to Ickwell Green. Two of the young men led the donkey down the lane, which left Sir Maxim and Kate with nothing to do but converse—if such a proper pastime were possible when surrounded by boisterous merrymakers.

Mr. Rowden and Polonius locked arms and danced a jig as they followed after the cart. By silent agreement they drew a deep breath and blew hard on their trumpets.

Sir Maxim winced at the discordant notes.

Turning and leaning close to his ear, Kate said, "That's my other brother, Polonius. He is considered to be a fine musician of the pianoforte, but the horn is beyond him."

Maxim couldn't keep the smile from his lips. "And of course Mr. McClintock is your father."

She nodded. "Of course!"

The clamour about them gradually died down to sporadic outbursts. The members of the procession seemed to be saving their exuberance for their triumphal entrance into Ickwell.

"Why, Katherina? Why are you telling me all this now?"

For a moment she didn't answer. And when she spoke, it was as if she'd not heard his question. "They call me Kate. It began as a jest, for I'm not at all shrewish."

"I know," he acknowledged. "You're quite even-tempered."

"That's because of my advanced age. I am considered quite on the shelf, don't you know. I'll be six-and-twenty before the year's end."

His eyes twinkled with the joy of these discoveries. "Your wisdom goes beyond a measure of time."

"Yet a woman isn't measured by wisdom, but by time. Society holds a beautiful young lady in higher esteem than a wizened but wise woman. 'O! call back yesterday, bid time return.'"

"Did your father instruct you in the writings of Shakespeare?"

"Papa?" Her voice quivered with amused astonishment. "He didn't have the patience for tutoring. He did, though, teach me all about gaming. As for the rest, I had very excellent governesses...when Papa had the funds to pay them. Managing a theatre is not always profitable."

"Then you've suffered destitution."

"Certainly not! This is the closest Papa's ever come to ruination." She gasped, disconcerted by her indiscreet lapse. "With luck, he'll make a thorough recovery."

"Is that why you came to Bedfordshire?"

She frowned at him. "We were going along so nicely, you and I—conversing amiably. Now you must be questing. I dislike being treated as a specimen of research. And do not try to deny you've made a study of me. You're not the only one who watches people." She looked about her. "Have you commented on the beauty of the day? A man with your talent for observation must have noted how much more vibrant the world seems since yesterday."

Maxim gazed around him as directed, but his attention came back to the object of his interest. "Might I call you Kate?"

"As long as you don't call me 'plain Kate,' 'bonny Kate,' or 'Kate the Cursed.'"

Again she won a smile from him, and he responded to her banter by saying, "'The prettiest Kate in Christendom.'"

She held her veil down as a breeze fluttered the diaphanous fabric. "You don't know that. I might have eyes that cross or a hairy wart on my forehead."

"Aha! Kate the Cursed. So that's why you hide behind the veil."

"La! sir, you've stumbled upon my secret," she remarked in a hoity-toity voice, teasing him back in kind. They laughed together.

Their mirth sparked a response in the others of the procession. The capering and cavorting began anew. Soon the merrymakers entered Ickwell Green singing, "Oh, here we are a Maying with a fa-la-la. Lads and lasses playing with a fa-la-la. A coin you'll be paying for a fa-la-la. As we go a Maying with a tra-la-la."

The revellers stopped at the first large house they came to—Colonel Buffard's. They began singing their song with a lusty relish. Out came the Colonel. He tossed a handful of coins up in the air.

Shouts of laughter and feminine shrieks erupted as the young men dashed after the coins. It mattered not if one of the coppers rolled under the skirt of someone's gown. Every last one was retrieved.

Bellamy Rowden stepped up to the cart. "Sir Maxim, as Lord of the May, you are required to kiss your lady for the tokens we've received."

Springing down from the cart, Maxim held up his arms to receive his lady. He smiled up at her, quite ready and willing to comply.

She proffered the hem of her gown, and said, "Kiss this, *signore*. It is part of me."

A chorus of hoots and jeers burst forth all around them.

He knelt on one knee and took the edge of her gown in one hand while he placed the other over his heart. "Dear Lady of the May, I cherish this and salute it as I would your rose-red lips." He kissed the hem to the delight of the crowd.

"That ain't doing the job proper, sir," the Colonel shouted. "In my day we knew how to buss a female."

The procession continued on. At the smithy's house, Sir Maxim plucked a posy from the cart, thinking he might cajole her with the offering, and presented it to Kate. He was allowed to kiss her little finger. Then at the following stop, she proffered her elbow. By the time they neared the village green, Maxim's initial disappointment had built into complete frustration. And he knew that by hook or by crook he'd kiss her long and hard on the lips so she'd know she'd been kissed.

At the tavern just across from the green, Kate hopped down from the cart before he could come around for her. He wondered what sort of trick she had in mind this time.

After the song and the receipt of the coins, Maxim gazed at her for a moment, not quite sure what he should do. Perhaps this time she would allow him to kiss her cheek.

When she grabbed his lapels and pulled him down to her, his surprise was patent. His eyes widened as she took his face in her hands and kissed him slowly and thoroughly.

The crowd cheered loud and long.

Breathless and feeling slightly embarrassed, Maxim at last stepped back. He stared at her. If he could have sat down he would have gladly done so, for his knees felt weak. Had he been willing to share such an intimate kiss with half the county, he'd have continued.

His gaze travelled to her mouth. He leaned forward, but the restraining pressure on his shoulder stayed him. A hand. Her brother's hand.

"Ka—that is, Contessa," Polonius said, trying for a masterful bass tone, "I can say with authority that Tony wouldn't like you making a spectacle of yourself. And I say don't overplay your role. Show a little decorum."

Upon hearing the last part of Polonius's remonstration, Bellamy Rowden chided him for being a spoilsport and asked, "What's the harm, dear chap? It's May, don't you know? Some dead fellow said, '...every lusty heart that is in any manner a lover, springeth and flourisheth in lusty deeds. For it giveth unto all lovers courage, that lusty month of May.'" He laughed at himself. "Even I've taken a paganish turn.

Let them live hand and glove today. Tomorrow they 'may repent at leisure.' ''

This declaration met with the approval of the crowd and Sir Maxim, who promptly gave Kate a look that promised he would finish what she'd begun.

CHAPTER TEN

PERCHED ATOP a specially devised throne, Kate tapped her foot to the time of the music as the dancers twirled and weaved in and out around the maypole. Though an awning shaded her from the sun, she fanned herself briskly. She knew the source of her increased warmth. A primeval desire stirred within her whenever Maxim was near. The sensation was quite pleasant, but surely it was most improper, and she wondered if she were indeed underbred to experience and savour the feeling.

Even though she held Maxim in the highest regard, she could not deny this peculiar stimulation which increased in intensity with each occasion when they shared each other's company—such as now. They sat practically touching shoulders. Her awareness manifested itself by the spirited way in which she fanned herself.

He leaned over from his place next to her. "Would you care for some of this rack punch? It's quite tasty." He sipped, then held the cup up to her. "Try it. Your lips look . . . parched."

Her tongue slid over her lower lip. She wished he would stop staring at her mouth. That particular attention kept reminding her of her wanton display of passion.

Without a thought to what she did, she downed a great gulp of punch. Then gasping and coughing, she stood and groped her way down the steps from the dias.

Sir Maxim was beside her before her foot touched the grass. He held her until she recovered sufficiently.

Wiping her eyes, she whispered, "That was strong punch!"

"I believe it is to be drunk in small measures." He chuckled. "You very nearly swallowed the whole cupful."

"Perhaps I was thirsty." Even to herself the suggestion sounded foolish. "The afternoon is becoming warm. Might we escape from our duties and see the sights of the fair?"

Glancing over his shoulder like a fellow conspirator, he said, "Hasten, before they notice we've taken French leave."

Hand in hand, they slipped away from the dancers and dashed for the canvas booths and stalls set up at the opposite end of the village green. They joined the press of people going to and fro. As they neared the May Fair, a stilt-walker loped by them. He stopped and turned about, then reached down and handed Maxim a bill of the play, announcing the performance of *Sodom and Gomorrah* by a travelling puppet-showman.

"There's a theatrical feat that is bound to prove interesting." Maxim pointed to the intriguing title on the handbill. "But I daresay we should avoid the place."

We would most likely find either your father or Mr. Rowden and your younger brother attending it.''

"Papa? Never! Polonius and Mr. Rowden's attendance is another matter entirely.''

"Shall *we* indulge in the whimsical?'' he asked with a devil-may-care look.

She regarded him with suspicion. "What have you in mind?''

"I've not been to a fair since my school days. It's May. Since we've got away let's make a thorough spree of it. We'll eschew everyone we know and everything we would normally do. Are you game?''

"You're talking to the daughter of a gamester, sir. I never refuse a challenge.''

One of the first amusements they came upon was a rope-dancer who drew a great crowd with his breathtaking use of swords. When the blades came deadly close to the performer's skin, Kate turned her face into Sir Maxim's shoulder.

"Begad!'' exclaimed Sir Maxim, sounding quite astonished.

"Did he draw blood?''

"No, I must be seeing things.''

Kate looked up at him. "What is it?''

"I thought I saw an old crony of mine, but that's impossible. He'd never leave London at the height of the Season.''

"Come along, then! We must eschew our friends, remember?''

Drawing him away from the crowd, Kate led Maxim to a stall emitting the juicy aroma of sizzling pork. Over a spit at the back of the makeshift kitchen, a large loin turned slowly. The banner at the foot of the stall declared that the pork came from the best farm in the county and was prepared by the best cook in all Christendom. They sampled the good woman's wares, coming away filled and content.

A juggler next caught their fancy, and was followed by a conjurer, who mystified his audience with amazing tricks. Only the sight of a merry-go-round drew Kate away from the magical arts.

She approached the whirling amusement with childlike enthusiasm, pulling Maxim along as she went. "Oh, look! Isn't it wonderful? I've always wanted to ride a merry-go-round. Only see how clever it is—wooden horses and sedan chairs."

"You want to ride that apparatus?" There was a dubious tone in his voice.

"I want us to ride it, yes. For the sake of whimsy."

Before he could resist further, she propelled him forward until they stood next to the attendant. The merry-go-round stopped. One man slid off and took a few staggering steps.

"Kate, the poor chap looks ready to cast up his accounts. Perhaps we should give this venture considerable thought before embarking rashly."

"Come, my Lord of the May, lead the way!" Kate hurried Maxim up to a carved horse, then she stepped into the pink sedan chair behind him.

Powered by a team of stout men pushing it, the merry-go-round jerked into motion, slowly building its speed to a bracing turn.

Invigorated by the breeze tickling her face, Kate allowed her veil to rise and fall at will. "Whee!" She held her arms out wide.

Maxim turned, ready to say something, then stared at her when the fabric over the upper half of her face lifted for a moment. He frowned. "Kate," he called between clenched teeth, "keep that veil down!" He glanced at the faces that seemed to spin by. "You mustn't be seen."

"Oh, pooh! I thought you wanted to see my hairy wart."

The merry-go-round began to slow. The individual faces of those watching became discernable.

"Begad! It's him again." Maxim turned round and searched the crowd. "Kate, keep your face covered. Get ready to jump off when I do."

"What is it? What's—"

"No questions. Just trust me." After another slow revolution, he leaped down and turned for her as she ran into him. Without a backward glance, he took her arm and plunged into the crowd. "Run, my dear. He may have seen us."

"Who?"

Maxim pushed his way through the stream of merrymakers, taking Kate with him. "You may well ask who he is, for he's your nemesis, Augustus Hazeltine—my closest friend and your most recent protector."

She nearly tripped to a stop. "You're joking! Why, I've never had a protector."

"But the Contessa D'Alessandria has had a protector—more protectors than you can count on your fingers and toes." He pulled her into a space between two canvas tents and held her facing him.

"Demme! He's seen us." Maxim crooked a finger under her chin. "Pardon the liberty, my dear, but...kiss me, Kate."

His mouth came down upon hers. And for a moment he forgot he was kissing her only in pretense. Deepening the embrace, he held her fast. Her unbridled response stirred his senses and perplexed his mind. How could a woman show passion so freely and yet *not* be a courtesan?

"Max, you fushty old bookman, what's that you're doing?" Augustus Hazeltine poked his beaked nose over Maxim's shoulder. "Here's a rare turnabout!" A strong vapour of brandy accompanied his words. "I'd have never thought it of you, Max. Have you forshaken the shtudy of life for the living of it?"

Raising his head but keeping Kate shielded, Maxim gazed up at his old crony. "Gustus! This is an unlooked-for surprise. What the deuce has brought you to Bedfordshire?"

"Melancholia." Augustus pulled out a flask, wiped the mouthpiece with his handkerchief and took a long swig of the contents. "The worsht case of—of the blue devils shince my youth. Remember? M' mother toshed out the governess—a pretty little thing with roshebud lips. Caught ush behind the stairs, don't you know. My shisters cried for weeks and called me a cad. And rightly so. Father shaid I was young and shent me to Scotland." He clapped a hand on Maxim's shoulder. "Had to tell you all about it. You're the closhest thing I've got to a brother."

"I've always been deuced fond of you, too, Gustus. But surely an old story about your youth could have waited until the end of the Season."

"I mish her."

"Who? The governess?"

Augustus snorted with laughter. "No, you looby! She's all of forty by now. I'm wearin' the willow for my dearest Contessa."

Maxim turned his shoulder a little more to screen Kate as she drew closer to him. "I thought you'd had enough of that lady. You must recall her constant demands and endless flirtations. How many times did you nearly have to meet some unknown jackanapes for the dubious sake of her honour...and yours? Besides, she never liked the cut of your coats."

After resorting to the flask again, Augustus said, "She was a cursh. All women are f-feckless creatures." He tapped the top of Kate's hat. "Who have you got here?"

"Who? Why, the most delightful minx in Bedfordshire." He rubbed Kate's shoulder. "But she's not for you, my buck. Be a good fellow and run along. I must be to my wooing."

"Musht be this cursed fresh air and bucolic revelry that's changed you, Max. You're not at all the shame as when I lasht clapped eyes on y'." Glancing at the merrymakers, Augustus squinted and swayed. "Maybe this is jusht what I need." He staggered off with a wave of the hand.

"Poor fellow," murmured Maxim.

"Sir, since your crony is safely fuddled," Kate said, calling his attention away from his departing friend, "as you decreed, you must be about your wooing."

He smiled at her, then stroked her jaw. "How remiss of me." He teased her lips with a feather-light kiss. "You're a plucky pullet—as game as they come." Glancing about, he offered his arm and led her out into the flow of May revellers.

"Pullet? A peagoose, perhaps. I daresay I'm not the delightful minx you say I am."

"Whatever makes you think you're not? Why, Kate, I've never enjoyed a female's company more than this day I've spent with you." He guided her over to a toyman selling trinkets. "Allow me to buy you a keepsake, milady. I'm sure it would be quite proper for the Lord of the May to give a present to his lady." He picked through the hawker's good. "This little drum? Or perhaps this whistling bird? What shall it be?"

Her glance wandered from the items held up for her inspection to the wares of the passing tinker, who saw her interest and began to peddle his handiwork.

"Here, missus," cried the tinker, polishing a thimble and holding it up for Kate's inspection, "have a look at this. It be silver. Made from a coin." He set the thimble down and took a pouch from his pocket. He drew out a piece of folded cloth and began to unwrap the treasure held within. A small silver ring caught the rays of the late-afternoon light. "It be for your babe's christening."

"I have no children." Kate took the ring and examined the intricate design and fine craftsmanship.

"Well, missus, if'n you have no babe, you might wear it yo'self till her comin'. See, how it slips on your little finger."

She held up her hand and admired the ring, then took it off. "It would be wasted on me," she said, holding it out for the tinker to take back.

"I think you should have it, Kate." Maxim closed his hand over hers. "It suits you."

"Aye, missus, and it be bad luck to take off a ring once it's on the finger. Me mother by law swears she got her nose wart from a cursed ring."

Maxim grinned at her and took the ring from her grasp, then slipped it on her little finger. He handed the tinker a generous remuneration. "You deserve it," he said to the fellow, winking.

"Thank you," Kate said softly.

"I hope it pleases you."

Smiling she replied, "I'm quite pleased with it. Now I shall be saved from nose warts."

"Though a medicinal charm it's a mere trifle."

"I will treasure it nonetheless." Her expression turned tender as she thought of babies, infant long-clothes and christenings. Did wishing make it come true, she wondered.

"'Ear, sir," the tinker muttered. "I'd watch your missus there."

"We're not wed," Maxim explained.

"Worse and worse, sir. I saw that same glimmer in me sweetheart's eye and now the chicks at home they number eight. Beware of a woman who wants babies, sir. It's marriage or nothin'."

Kate hurried away, laughing. Amusement was the only answer in the face of such a mortifying statement. The tinker possessed the gift of a soothsayer. He could see clear through to her heart, but did he have to proclaim it to the world?

"Wait up," called Maxim. Just as he caught hold of her, he exclaimed, "Zounds!" Then pushed her behind him. "Gustus is fast at hand."

"Max! Max, I've looked everywhere for you. And everywhere I go I hear 'the Contessha did thish' or 'the Contessha shaid that.' The people of thish village can shpeak of nothin' elsh. I'm haunted by the woman. They sheem to think the Contessha D'Alesshandria ish here in the neighbourhood. It's ridiculous, of courshe."

"Yes, ridiculous! You mustn't heed them." Maxim held his arms behind him, giving Kate the cover she needed. "Wouldn't I tell you if she were here?"

Augustus laughed drunkenly. "They shay she hash a tendre for you. It mus' be a jest. You know all about books, Max, but nothin' about women. Beshides, you wouldn't carry on with her behind my back. Very unshportsmanlike."

"The Contessa is in Ireland, Gustus. Rest easy. You should retire to an inn to sleep away your sorry state."

"Fushty fellow. I need diversion and this fair ish jusht the thing." He peered around Sir Maxim's shoulder. "Aha! Who's that behind you? Make a clean breasht of it, you came here t' the wilds of nowhere to dally with the wenches. First it's one and now another. There's shtill hope for you!"

Maxim backed away. "I knew I couldn't hide anything from you, Gustus." He glanced over his shoulder, then gave his friend a lecherous grin. "You must excuse me. Sorry to be boorish, but I can't keep the wench waiting. And I must see how Lucy fares."

"Not to worry 'bout her. Shome chap's guardin' her from any who'd approach. Tried to pay my respec's, but he'd have none of it. Well, I don't blame 'im. I wouldn't let a man in my—" he shook his head as if to clear it "—my condition near my shishter, either. Must be off." He strode away with a crooked gait, needing the support of his walking stick to hold him up.

"Come along, Kate," Maxim said, putting his arm around her and hustling her away, "we've got to hide you until it gets dark. Sooner or later someone is going to tell Gustus that the Contessa and I have been together all day... that the Contessa is a guest of Squire Colley."

"What would your friend do if he me found out?"

"Most likely offer you an indecent proposal. But he's sure to say or do something to ruin it all. My dear, we need to come up with a plan to waylay him."

Unfortunately they were waylaid themselves by the poet Rufus Sayer. "Contessa! I've searched everywhere for you," he said dramatically as he came upon them. "When all was lost the fates decreed that I should have the good fortune to find you." He paused importantly. "It's finished. My humble effort—forty-seven copperplate-written pages—is at last completed. I would like to read it to you if I might have a moment of your time."

"Perhaps later," Maxim said, taking Kate's arm.

She stayed him and courteously gave her attention to the poet. "I daresay you've laboured night and day, Mr. Sayer. And I am deeply grateful. But such a work—you did say it was to be an ode?"

"An epic, ma'am. I promised you an epic. It's entitled *The Death of a Rose.*" He tore off his battered hat and ruffled his red hair. "I had a dashed awful time coming up with enough words, but I did it! Last night I nearly tossed it all away, though." He looked shamefaced. "I couldn't think of the proper word or phrase to rhyme with gazelle."

"Gazelle?" Maxim glared at him. "Try 'go to—'"

"—the *well*," Kate suggested, pinching Maxim's arm.

"I thought of 'fairies will tell,'" said Mr. Sayer, sounding rather smug.

"I'm sure you've written a lovely epic," Kate said politely. "And I should be delighted to read it…all of the way through. But this is hardly the place for it, and the sun *is* beginning to set. If you would be so kind as to bring it to the manor tomorrow I might read it then."

"I shall stay awake thinking of you, Contessa, until we meet again." Mr. Sayer bowed, then hurried away as if he were chasing the muse.

"Come," Maxim said, taking Kate's hand, "before some other chucklehead accosts us."

They headed for a stand of trees next to the smithy. She settled on a bench beneath the spreading foliage, while he paced, deep in thought.

After a time, he stopped abruptly before her. "Kate, I don't know all there is to know about you or your circumstances, but I do know this—"

"Yes?"

"You cannot continue as the Contessa—at least not here. You must see that someone's bound to come along and know you for a fraud." He cursed under his breath and scowled at her. "Confound it, Kate, it's dashed awkward speaking to you about a serious subject when you're draped in that veil. I daresay I should be used to it by now, but I'm not." He sat down next to her and took hold of the netting. "May I?"

She did not draw away.

Lifting the gauze slowly, he was silent as he revealed first her slender nose, then her eyes—beautiful eyes—and brows. "Begad, Kate, you're beautiful."

"Thank you, Maxim." Embarrassed, she began to look down.

He cupped her chin with his hand. "Let me look at you a moment."

Her eyes weren't blue, but green. Not a fiery, temperamental green, but a soft, fresh verdant hue, like a valley in the springtime. Her dark lashes were a perfect frame.

She closed her eyes. It seemed natural that he oblige by kissing her.

"I think I hear Gustus coming," he murmured, his lips only inches from hers. "Kiss me, Kate," he said huskily. His thoughts fled before the surge of his emotions. He only wanted to explore the depths of her mouth and find the goodness deep within her.

"Maxim," she whispered, pulling back from him, "I'm sure this is improper. I know I *feel* improper. What must you think of me?"

He couldn't answer her. To his amazement, he found that nothing seemed quite clear. What the deuce was wrong with him?

"My dear girl," he said, trailing his fingers down her throat, "you feel quite proper to me. And I think... I know you have the finest eyes in His Majesty's kingdom." He wrapped a wisp of her hair around his finger. "Shall I ever see you without something covering your head?"

"I misdoubt it. Papa has great plans that I dare not overset." She moved from him and strolled to the side of a tree, leaning her head against it. "I'm in quite a fix. There will be no easy way out."

"Kate, there has to be—" He broke off. The sounds of a commotion drew his attention, and he cursed. "Gustus? Not again." His impatience carried in his voice. "My dear, you must hide—once more."

She ducked behind the tree, but peeped out to say, "Behold the chuckleheads!"

In the clutches of Polonius and Mr. Rowden, Augustus fought for his freedom. "Let me go, louts! Thish's no way to handle a gentleman." He tried to shake his escorts off. "Mosht determined pair of bailiffs I've had the mishfortune to meet. Give me back m' purse!"

"Gentlemen!" Maxim called as they tried hauling their captive into the smithy's. "Wait just a moment! What's the to-do?"

Mr. Rowden turned, looking the soul of righteous indignation, and said, "This blackguard has defamed the name of a lady, whom my friend here and I hold in high esteem. We've chosen this out-of-the-way place to bring him to his senses. Proverbs 13:24—'He that spareth his rod hateth his son: but he that loveth him chasteneth him betimes.'"

"Did you hear that, Max? They're goin' to cane me!" Augustus appeared more irate than frightened.

"Actually," said Polonius, "we planned to plunge his head a few times into the smithy's water barrel."

"Hear that?" Augustus seemed satisfied with the admission. "They're plotting my death by drowning. My coat will be ruined!"

"Gustus, do be quiet," Maxim said with exasperation. "You should never come into the country, not unless you bring your tailor. Old friend, it's time you went back to Town. Mr. Rowden, would you be kind enough to ride into Biggleswade and order a posting chaise? Have them send it over immediately."

The cleric frowned. "Don't let him go. He's said such things that he's inflamed half the village. There was talk of resorting to the pillory. 'A fool's mouth is his destruction'—Proverbs 18.7." He went off into the gathering twilight.

"Begad, what did he mean by that?" Augustus seemed to be coming to his senses.

"You're a fool, Gustus," Maxim said. "You repine for a woman who's made you a cuckold. The Contessa D'Alessandria carries another man's child."

Polonius held Augustus, but the older man made no outward display of emotion. He only sucked on his lip.

Maxim clapped his friend upon the shoulder, just like he'd done since their days at Oxford. "I'd rather you heard it from me than from any of the many who'll boast that it was theirs but then decline to claim it."

"Sho that's why she went to Ireland?" Augustus swore. "I very nearly named a new arrangement of my cravat after her. Begad, I would look the fool then."

"Return to Town," Maxim said, "and attend the opera, the balls, and Almack's. Find a genteel young lady to pay court to and give the gossips something to twitter about."

"I don't like those Friday-faced heiresshes or those self-important beauties. A woman with shtyle is jusht the ticket."

Maxim's expression softened. "Find a lady you're at ease with. Then, with luck, you'll find her pleasing of face and figure."

"It's remarkable how thish fresh country air has cleared away the cobwebs in your head. There's hope for you yet." Augustus smiled weakly, then slumped down on the bench and fell asleep.

Polonius approached Maxim and whispered, "You know about the Contessa?"

"Your sister's secret is safe with me." Sir Maxim's serious mien gave added significance to his words.

"Where's the, ah, Contessa?" Polonius whispered, glancing nervously at Augustus.

"I'm here," Kate said, stepping out from behind the tree. She regarded Maxim warmly. "You're quite a fine friend. You did him a kindness, one that required pluck."

"He'd have done the same."

Polonius looked from one to the other, then took a few paces and lowered his sister's veil. "What's been afoot here?" He drew her aside. "Papa will be displeased. A player never steps out of character until the close of the last scene."

An uncomfortable silence settled between them and only the arrival of Mr. Rowden a few minutes later stirred them from their respective reveries.

"The chaise is waiting on the other side of the green," the cleric said. "There's such a press of people that the way is quite impassable. The promised fireworks display has drawn every soul from this part of the county." He bowed to Kate. "They await the presence of the Lord and Lady of the May. Can't begin without you."

Maxim looked uneasily at his slumbering friend.

"Mr. Rowden and I will tend to him, sir," Polonius said, "if you would see that the Contessa is returned safely to her bodyguard. He will escort her back to the manor."

"It shall be as you wish it, sir," Maxim said, "but you need not fear while she's in my company." He gave Polonius a pointed look. "Would you be so kind as to see that my friend is given a private parlour at the White Hart Inn? I'll be by later to see him on his way to London."

Polonius seemed relieved. With a lighthearted smile, he hoisted Augustus up and wrapped one of the fellow's arms around his shoulder while Mr. Rowden took the other side. Dragging the inebriated man between them, they trudged across the green.

"Shall we go?" Maxim properly offered Kate his arm. Stepping from the darkly shadowed twilight beneath the trees to the torch-lit green was like returning from a dream world.

She remained quiet until just before reaching the dais. "In years to come," she said softly, "I'll remember this day and the adventures we've shared."

"You speak as if your life is ending." He squeezed her hand. "You'll have many more adventures, I promise you."

"A lady's companion doesn't have adventures. And my life as the Contessa is near its end." She gave him a wistful little smile, which turned heartrending when a single tear slid down her cheek. Turning away from him, she mounted the dais and somehow managed to receive with composure the tribute of the May Day revellers.

Maxim took his place at her side and unobtrusively held her hand. He waved at the crowd as they shouted out such things as, "Long live the Lord and Lady of the May! Huzzah! Sir Maxim! Long live the Contessa!"

At that particular cry, a disturbance erupted from the rear of the crowd, but ceased abruptly when Polonius knocked Augustus on the head with his own walking stick.

"Long live the Contessa," the crowd cheered. "Long may the Lord and Lady of the May be happy!"

The firework display came to brilliant life, lighting the faces of the merrymakers. Its fiery sparkle lasted a short time, then faded away to nothingness. After the smoke cleared, only the memory of its animation remained.

Some vital part inside of Kate felt as if it too were fading away. She wanted to hold on to it, but it was going...and she feared she would never have it again.

CHAPTER ELEVEN

"KATHERINA, THIS IS a serious matter. When Polonius told me the whole of it I could scarcely believe it of you." Henry McClintock stood with his back to the drawing-room fireplace, alternating warming his hands and spreading the tails of his coat. "It saddens me beyond words to discover the necessity of this interview."

She, too, had hoped to avoid it, but her father had waited for her on the front steps of the manor. When she'd returned from Ickwell with Anthony and Lucy, she knew there would be no escape even though the hour was late. And so it was that they now faced each other surrounded by the Squire's opulent trappings.

"Though your life has been sheltered from the stage," he stated, "still you should know that a player of parts never abdicates his role until the conclusion of the piece. You've behaved foolishly, but succumbing to a case of the megrims will hardly benefit us." He scowled at the *JGC* woven into the carpet. "Purse-proud pup," he muttered, then glanced up in time to catch his daughter with the beginnings of a smile on her lips. "That's better, child. As I see it, we've had a minor setback."

"Sir Maxim suggested—"

"*Sir Maxim* suggested! Who invited the fellow to meddle in our concerns?"

"Sir Maxim suggested," Kate continued as if her father had not spoken, "that it would be best to leave before the game's up. He fears that his friend may have said even more than we suspect. If the gossips get even a hint of something irregular they're apt to stumble upon our pretense." She gazed calmly at him from her place on the sofa.

"The only item the gossips are likely to remark upon is that the Contessa and Sir Maxim were seen cuddling in public." He glared at his daughter. "Had you not been so thoroughly occupied you might have noticed that I, too, was among the throng at the fair."

"Papa, that indiscretion can be explained," she said, flushing a little. "Sir Maxim did not want his friend to see my face."

"So, being a gentleman, he covered it with his own. How thoughtful of him."

"He was trying to protect me. He fears what might happen should we be discovered." These same concerns weighed with her also. She no longer feared being unmasked, but failure would mean all had been for naught. And with discovery there would surely be repercussions. "Papa, the Squire seems to be the sort of man who would find a certain satisfaction in transporting a man he thought had wronged him. I don't know what crime we've committed—we've certainly not swindled anyone of their money—but I daresay the Squire would invent a law so he might accuse us of breaking it. The offense of hoodwinking for the purpose of financial gain is sure to land us in gaol."

"Nonsense. You are allowing your thoughts to be overtaken by fancy." Henry's brow wrinkled and he appeared absorbed in working through a particular matter. "I had planned to stay at the manor for at least another fortnight. Today's May Fair opened many more opportunities for me. If we departed now, it would take quite some time to reestablish ourselves elsewhere."

"The odds of being discovered are great—too great to risk continuing as we are. It would be wise to flee while we still have our freedom to do so."

"Nonetheless, my dear, I am willing to bet that our luck has not run out just yet. Of course, fate is capricious and one never knows what is around the next corner. I've this feeling, though, that there are matters still to be settled." He joined her on the sofa and took her hands in his warm clasp. "Polonius is worried that you may no longer be heart-whole." He gazed into her eyes. "Kate, when one embarks on a venture such as this, it is best to remember that it is *all* make-believe. You've played a part, and you've played your part well. Perhaps too well. Is the gentleman enamoured with who you are or who you seem to be? Are your inclinations your own or those you merely think to be your own?"

Kate felt the sting of tears nettle her eyes. "I . . . I don't know the answers, Papa. I've changed so that I scarcely recognize myself anymore. I used to accept life as it came, content to find peace in a lacklustre existence. I troubled no one and no one troubled me— amiable is how I've been known. Now, I want more than what a spinster can expect as her fair portion. Is it wrong for a woman to desire children? How many years must one stay on the shelf before one's thought too old for love? Must a female simply resign herself to the fate Society has relegated her to?''

"Dear, oh dear, oh dear," Henry said, shaking his head, "are your inclinations so firmly fixed? It was only one kiss, after all. He didn't..."

The festering sore of self-condemnation made itself felt. Should she confess her numerous indiscretions? Even her father's phlegmatic philosophy, engendered by the theatrical life, could not ease her conscience. She had allowed Sir Maxim liberties that only a woman of low repute or a betrothed lady would grant, and she was neither. How supreme the mortification of informing one's father that his beloved daughter was without a sense of propriety or even moral preservation. The question of her inclinations paled when weighed against her sense of guilt. Besides, would a gentleman be inclined to offer for a dowerless woman who'd thrown herself at him?

"Papa, my desires are not always what they should be. I seem to want what is forbidden."

"Marriage is never forbidden, no matter the age, to any who desire it. Of course there are many who would snigger if a man of my years married, particularly if the woman concerned could no longer bear children. But that is a delicate matter which we need not trouble ourselves discussing." Henry locked his hands before him and tapped his thumbs together. "Should I be expecting a visit from your particular gentleman? Would you be favourably receptive to an offer of marriage?"

"Marriage? Impossible! It will always be a falling star on my horizon, just out of reach." She stood abruptly. She would never blame him for gambling away her marriage portion, small though it may have been. Without a dowry she was considered worthless. Penniless spinsters did not marry. Routed by her thoughts, she hastened to the door, but paused to cast her father a brave smile. "Do not bide here, Papa, waiting for a particular gentleman to seek you out. If I am wanted, I daresay that nuptials would not enter into the arrangement."

"Katherina! Remember you're gently bred."

But would she be gently wed before she was not-so-gently taken to bed, she wondered.

"I try to remember, sir." She pulled open the door and then, in an attitude of defeat, leaned her head upon it. "I must be overtired. It's been a long and eventful day. Goodnight, Papa." She jerked down her veil as she walked out.

She moved through the Grand Hall with sluggish steps. How dismal the future looked. She felt positively hagged when she thought of the years ahead. Catching her image in a decorative pier glass, she paused when she saw the dejected slump in her posture. Resolutely she straightened up and squared her shoulders.

This morbidity would simply not do. Whatever the prospect on her horizon, she would view it with an eye focused only on that which was bright and promising. Surely there were many things an unmarried lady could do. No one had thought of them all as yet, which was why females stayed confined to the strictures placed upon them.

In time her unfulfilled dreams would fall aside, to be replaced by the propitious aspirations of a mature lady. She would become a travelling companion, only contracting for situations that offered extensive trips abroad. Perhaps she would write about her travels, which seemed a respectable way to become notorious.

Kate smiled as she began to climb the stairs. Her confidence dipped at the sight of the Squire creeping down the steps towards her.

"Contessa," he whispered loudly, "I must speak to you privately. Come to the library with me."

"I am on my way up to bed, *signore*. Might this matter wait until tomorrow?"

At the mention of bed, the Squire's black eye closed and his other widened as if he were trying to wink and then he grinned lecherously. "The hour is not so very late. Just a moment of your time, I beg you."

She preceded him into the library. Turning, she found him fast upon her, so close she could smell the remnants of his dinner on his breath—particularly the onions and cabbage. A parlour chair seemed a safe refuge and she took it.

"You needn't be coy with me now that we're alone," he said, dragging a chair close to hers. He sat down and positioned himself so that their knees touched.

She edged away from him.

"My dearest Contessa, your assumption of modesty is a continual source of amusement to me. But your airs are wasted. I know who you are and what you are."

Kate sat very still, waiting.

"Contessa, you are a woman of vast experience and I am a man of the world. I know how the game is played."

"Game?" she asked, her voice low and unsure. "You Englishmen confuse me. I play no games. They fatigue me."

He grinned at her. "By the time we're finished, you'll be exhausted. I always leave my women breathless and warm—very warm."

Grimacing, she said, "It does not sound pleasant. I do not think I want to play your game, sir. Pray, excuse me."

He caught her arm as she tried to leave. "You've played before. You'll do so again with me, my sweet bird of pleasure." Then he licked his lips and swallowed. "We both know the rules. I give you a gift and you . . . diddle with me. A favour for a favour. Now, don't act so surprised."

How strange, she thought, that her brothers shouldn't be nearby acting as chaperon when she really needed one. Rallying her ingenuity and courage, she faced the Squire in the same coquettish manner she thought the real Contessa might use. "You wish to give me a gift? What is it? I must warn you that I am used to receiving the very best of everything. Do not insult me with a trinket of no value." Perhaps she could discourage him if the price were too high.

The Squire squeezed her knee, then patted her leg confidently.

Thoroughly affronted, she sprang to her feet and, feeling a strong desire to strike him, forced herself to restrain from any obvious outburst of temper. Not even an amiable female would tolerate such liberties as his. She vowed he would yet live to rue his actions.

"*Signore,* you must not move too quickly." She whacked his hand smartly with her fan.

He nursed the back of his hand. "Quickly! I've waited weeks to have you. No woman has ever kept me dangling so blasted long before. And not one kiss have I got for my patience." He began to loosen his cravat. "Well, I ain't waiting any longer."

"Your mother might come upon us at an awkward moment." These words had the effect she knew they would.

Glancing uneasily at the door, he asked, "Did you hear something?"

"Did you hear it also?" she asked, not having heard anything herself. "I must leave before we are discovered." She hurried for her escape.

"Wait!" He moved quicker than she and grabbed her by the arm. "Take this. I'll come to your room later, at midnight. A favour for a favour, my dear Contessa."

She looked down at the very heavy gold and ruby necklace he held out to her. When she would not take it, he forced it into her hand. She nearly threw it back at him, but he began to move upon her with amorous intent. As fast as she could, she darted from the room and hurried up the stairs.

"I'll not be able to contain my eagerness either, my sweet," the Squire called after her. "Hurry and make yourself ready to receive me fully."

Kate plunged breathlessly into her room and slammed the door behind her, bolting it. He'd have to force his way through to get at her, and she'd do him an injury before she'd allow him to touch her. She very nearly cast the necklace into the fire, but, just in time, the farcical nature of the situation struck her.

She took perverse satisfaction from the realization that the Squire would be thoroughly frustrated when he found the way barred to him. But to ensure her complete safety she sent her maid for Anthony. She would not be sleeping alone that night, not without a protector. However, the role would hardly be the one the Squire had envisioned.

With the gift of an active imagination, Kate could see in her mind's eye the preparations that the Squire was surely engaged in for their tryst. And all for naught, she mused with a smile.

IN THE OPPOSITE WING of the manor the Squire stood in his drawers poised before the cheval glass as his valet loosened his Apollo corset. "Give me plenty of room to breath," the Squire ordered. "My exertions tonight will be above the ordinary." He gazed at himself, turning this way and that. "I might decide to do away with the corset altogether. I'll be wanting to give it my all. Then again, if I can manage to keep my shirt on, the Contessa will not remark upon my stays. Besides, if the Prince Regent can wear them, I daresay I should also be allowed the same considerations." He slapped his midsection. "I've the look of a young field-worker, have I not?"

The valet readily agreed.

Sitting at his dressing table, the Squire allowed his man to groom and shave him. He was thus engaged when his mother stormed into his room unannounced. The Squire, with lather covering half his face, sprang up and drew his dressing gown together. "What the devil is the meaning of this, Mother?" he asked, flushing a little at being caught in his apparent preparations.

"My son, I came to you the *instant* I made the discovery. We've been robbed! My favourite gold and ruby necklace is missing."

The Squire's previous flush paled. Though obviously distressed and in need of attention, he dismissed his valet. "Are you quite sure you've not misplaced it, Mama?"

"I've looked in all my jewel chests, but it isn't in any of them. How providential that I was counting my baubles today—I always do so when I'm unhappy— for I might not have taken note of the theft." She glanced at him curiously. "Do you always go to such lengths when readying yourself for bed?"

He wiped the lather from his face. "I like to maintain my appearance at all times." He cleared his throat. "About your necklace, Mama. I—I daresay it will turn up by morning. There's nothing to fret about. It was doubtlessly mislaid somewhere."

"Mislaid! Stolen, you mean! And by those gypsies."

"What gypsies?" He looked hopeful, ready to grasp at any straw offered.

"Why those foreigners we have living with us in this very house. They say they are Italian, but I believe them to be gypsies."

He groaned. "Mama, they're people of the theatre. You like the theatre, remember?"

"Actors are no better than gypsies."

"But she's a songstress." His voice cracked in desperation as he glanced at the clock.

"No matter. They're all the same. Thieves and murderers!" She collapsed on a chair, which creaked ominously from her assault. "I took her to my bosom and just see how she has repaid me."

"Who? The Contessa?"

She clenched her fist over her meager breast. "Of course, the Contessa! Who else would serve me such a trick? I gave her shelter when no one else would. I introduced her to my friends and neighbours. I took her to all the parties. I did all this out of the goodness of my heart and see what she has done in return. Taken my gold and ruby necklace!"

"Mama, you mustn't upset yourself. To accuse the Contessa is unjust."

"Unjust? I invited that woman here, thinking how pleasant it would be to have the famous songstress for a guest. She's sung only once! My friends pity me now because you've made a cake of yourself over her. No word of her being here has reached the newspapers in Town. No one of importance knows she is staying with us. What's the good of having her? She's outstayed her usefulness. And now she's stolen my necklace. That, sir, is unjust!''

"How can you be so sure that the Contessa has taken your necklace?''

"Who else would do such a dreadful thing?''

He swallowed hard. "Maybe you forgot you lent it to her?''

Her eyes bulged with the force of her outrage. "Have you lost your senses completely? Send for the constable at once! I want that thief taken up!''

"Mother, it is late. In the morning I'll look into the matter.''

"I demand that she be seized now! By morning she'll likely be gone.''

Glancing at the clock, ticking steadily onward to midnight, he took his mother by the arm and marched her to the door. "In the morning I shall find your necklace and return it to you. Until then…goodnight, madam!''

"If you refuse to honour my wishes this very minute, I'll go for the constable myself.''

"Go to bed, Mother!'' He closed the door in her face.

Mrs. Colley pounded on the door, but to no avail. With a steely glint of determination in her eye, she ambled down the corridor and returned to her room. There she rang long and hard for her maid. Soon afterwards a messenger was dispatched.

The mistress of the house went down to the Grand Salon to await the coming of the constable. On the stairs she met Sir Maxim coming up.

"I must warn you, sir," she said. "We've robbers in this house. My son will not heed me, but you are not so besotted. Guard your sister, our precious Lucy, from that woman and her tricks."

"What woman?"

"The Contessa D'Alessandria is a thief." Her voice tolled out like a bell of doom. "I've sent for the constable and within the hour I shall see her delivered to the lock-up in Biggleswade. Then when my son next sees her, he will be acting as the magistrate and all her misdeeds will come to light." She shrank back from the angry look in his eyes. "Why, sir, whatever is the matter? Dear Lucy will be safe at last from that wicked woman."

Sir Maxim cursed, then took the stairs two at a time.

CHAPTER TWELVE

A SURREPTITIOUS TAP-TAP fell upon the Contessa's chamber door. Unconsciously, Kate drew her dressing gown together and held it tight at the neck. Backing away from the door, she cast a questioning glance at her brother, who shook his head decisively.

He signalled for her to remain quiet, then directed her to hide in the adjoining dressing room. But she defiantly tiptoed across to the nearby Louis XVI screen and concealed herself behind it.

Someone rattled the door handle. "Dash it, Kate," Sir Maxim called through the wood panels, "let me in!"

She darted from her cover and threw back the bolt. "Maxim? Is that you?" Opening the door wide, she peered out into the dimly lit corridor and said, "Do not say that you, too, have come to seduce me. I had thought better of your sensibilities. This is hardly the time for such nonsense. Go away!"

He eased by her without a word and locked the door after him. "My dear, *if*—or when—I come to you," he murmured to Kate, "there will be no nonsense. How very pleasing you look bareheaded." He touched her dark curls, then turned to face Anthony. "I'm the bearer of bad news. It would seem that Mrs. Colley has overstepped her bounds. She's summoned the constable.''

Anthony swore soundly and sat down with a defeated air. ''Are you quite sure? Have they found Kate out?''

''Mrs. Colley thinks the Contessa is a thief.'' Sir Maxim glanced around the ornately furnished room. ''What the dickens she imagines someone would want to take from this place escapes me, but she is pursuing the matter to the fullest extent. Which means,'' he said, taking Kate by the shoulders, ''that you must leave.''

''But my father hasn't completed his business here,'' she said, shrugging out of his hold.

''I've just come from speaking with him and he is in full agreement with me. He deems the risks have become too great to stay longer.'' Sir Maxim pulled a folded sheet of paper from inside his waistcoat. He handed this to Anthony, who took it gingerly.

Reading over her brother's shoulder, Kate at first narrowed her eyes suspiciously, then felt them widen with each phrase of her father's hastily scrawled note. '' 'Join you in a week—' '' she repeated aloud, '' 'in Buckinghamshire. Sir M. will be your host until then. Leave you in his capable hands.' '' She stared at Sir Maxim. ''What is the meaning of this?''

''The meaning is plain enough. Your father has entrusted your care to me. He and Polonius have gone into hiding.''

''This will not do. I'm too old for a guardian.''

He smiled at her in evident good humour. His dimples peeped out. ''Then think of me as your protector... but not *that* sort of protector," he added, after her irate gasp.

"Tony will see to my welfare," she retorted.

Anthony sighed and shook his head wearily. "This is hardly the time to be sparring with words. The two of you may continue your dispute later. Kate, please dress, then pack only what you can carry yourself. Sir," he said, giving him an offhand salute, "I place myself under your command."

"I appreciate your cheerful support—under these unusual circumstances," Maxim said. "Take your sister to Lucy's bedchamber as soon as she is ready to leave. The hue and cry may be given at any moment so do hurry." Without giving Kate a glance, he left the chamber with the air of a man still burdened with much to do.

For a moment Kate stared after him. How was she to proceed as an adventuresome spinster when placed under his charge? She'd hoped to avoid him, and thus eventually recover from her predilection for him. She felt quite sure that she'd live to regret placing herself under his obligation. How did the Squire phrase it? A favour for a favour.

The recollection brought to mind that very soon the Squire would be coming to the Contessa's chamber. Kate dashed into the dressing room. In the midst of squirming into a gown and throwing linens, stockings, nightgowns and other articles into a bandbox, Kate instructed Anthony to write her maid a letter of dismissal and include a generous amount for service and coach fare.

"Write that she may have anything which I leave behind," she added, as she finished pulling on her half boots, "*except* for this." She laid the gold and ruby necklace on the dressing table. "Even the Squire will understand the meaning when he finds I've gone without it."

"We'd better leave before he gets here."

Glancing about the room, Kate smiled mischievously. "Shall we set the stage first?" She threw back the covers on the bed and fluffed the pillows, then spilled a bottle of scent over all.

Anthony doused the candles except for the one closest to the bed. A distant tower clock began to toll the hour just as he scooped up Kate's mantel and bandbox and pushed her into the dressing room.

"We'll wait in here until he comes," he whispered, "then slip out by the other door when all's clear."

Hardly had they gotten into the dressing room before a stealthful scratch sounded at the bedchamber door. Peeking out the slight opening, Kate and Anthony watched as the Squire crept into the room.

"Contessa," he cooed. "My sweet plum of delight, where are you?" He glanced at the dressing-room door. "Don't keep me waiting long." Spying his mother's gold and ruby necklace on a nearby table, he snatched it up and fondled it. With the necklace in hand, he bounded over to the bed and hopped in. His dressing gown sailed out before he yanked the draperies closed about the bed and waited, giggling in anticipation.

After a moment he poked his head out and called, "I'm ready to pleasure you. Come to me, Contessa."

AT A QUARTER TO MIDNIGHT, Sir Maxim entered the
Grand Salon along with the constable, a sleepy-eyed
fellow in dishevelled clothes. Sir Maxim clapped the
man on the back and commended him on his dili-
gence and strong sense of duty. "For it's not every
official of the law who'd fall out of bed at a moment's notice."

The constable yawned and rubbed his face. "I don't
like to keep the Squire waitin'. He bein' the magistrate and all."

"Very proper sentiments," commented Sir Maxim.
"You're a remarkably fine fellow, and so I shall tell
the Squire."

"It was I who summoned you here," Mrs. Colley
said to the constable. "I hope you will regard my
wishes as highly as you do the Squire's. I desire that
you take up a person who has stolen a very costly
necklace of mine."

"Who is this person, ma'am?" The constable appeared more alert at the mention of stolen jewels.

"The Contessa D'Alessandria of the Kingdom of
Sardinia," Mrs. Colley replied, evidently relishing the
denouncement.

The constable gasped.

"Are you quite sure, ma'am?" Sir Maxim asked.
He wasn't questioning Kate's innocence. He only
wanted to give her enough time to seek refuge in
Lucy's room.

"Do you doubt my word?" Mrs. Colley swung
about and glared at him.

"Not at all, madam, but have you questioned all
your servants? Your maid might have—"

"My maid has been with me for years and years. She has never given me cause to suspect her honesty or loyalty."

Sir Maxim decided to try another track. "Perhaps a stranger gained entry into the manor and—"

"The only stranger to have wheedled her way into this house is the Contessa. Constable, do your duty," Mrs. Colley said, pointing dramatically to the door. "Follow me!"

After a stately ascent of the staircase, like an executioner's march, they stood before the Contessa's suite of rooms. The constable scratched his head and shuffled his feet uneasily. Mrs. Colley impatiently tapped her foot. Sir Maxim whispered a prayer for divine intervention.

"Well?" Mrs. Colley demanded.

"Are you wantin' me to batter down the door?" The constable presented his stout shoulder.

Sir Maxim took hold of the door handle and slowly inched the opening wider. He peered about, hoping that Kate had made her escape. A dressing gown abandoned by the bed gave him pause.

"What are you waiting for?" Mrs. Colley whispered.

"Looks to be asleep," the constable muttered, peeking over Sir Maxim's shoulder. Pushing by, the constable tiptoed forward.

A giggle from the bed caught their attention. The constable froze in his tracks. But the lady of the house swept past him and flung back the draperies, holding them to the side.

With lips puckered and eyes closed, the Squire lay bare, trailing the ruby and gold necklace across his sparsely haired, oily chest. "You give to me and I'll give to you—a favour for a favour."

It was then that Mrs. Colley looked in the bed. "Jethro Gillingham!"

The Squire's eyes shot open. Caught with the goods, he thrust them behind his back. He squirmed as the gems cut into his flesh. He then recalled his state of undress. Grabbing for the sheet, he tried to cover the display of his manly virtues.

At the sight of his stunned mother's face, he squealed. She wailed. In union, mother and son caterwauled until they both turned red.

Her eyes grew as round as saucers, then she collapsed in a swoon. The constable caught her before she hit the floor, but the weight of her ample hips pulled them both down. She fell heavily upon him.

"Get this sow off me!" the constable cried.

Holding his discarded Apollo corset before him, the Squire rapped the constable upon the head. "Mind how you speak of m' mother." He snatched the dressing gown from the floor and shrugged into it. Sucking in his midsection to secure the fastenings, he glanced about with a confused expression. "Where's the Contessa? What the deuce is the meaning of this intrusion?"

Pulling the constable from beneath Mrs. Colley's inert form, Sir Maxim remarked, "Your good mother thought—" he paused to wrestle with a smile "—she was exposing a criminal."

The Squire drew the front of his dressing gown more tightly together. "Do I look like a criminal?" he demanded, glaring down at the constable. "How dare you intrude upon me at such a delicate moment!"

"Pardon, Squire, how was I to know you'd be in the Contessa's bed?"

Apparently liking the gist of the constable's words, the Squire swelled his chest and sauntered about the room as if it were his rightful domain. "My private affairs are none of your concern."

The constable rummaged through the sheets. Holding the necklace betwixt his thumb and finger, he examined it at arm's length. "Is this the missing article reported stolen by your mother?" the constable ventured.

"Ha! Much you know about it, you ignorant fool," the Squire exclaimed, grabbing the necklace. He turned away and pocketed it in his dressing gown, then, trying to get out the door, tripped over his mother's legs. "Ring for her maid! What sort of man are you to leave the poor woman thusly?"

Sir Maxim offered to fetch the lady's maid. He knew if he stayed much longer in the same room as the Squire he would darken the fellow's daylights again. Though having no right to act on Kate's behalf, he longed to squelch the pretensions of the overblown, pubescent puffer.

Before Sir Maxim could quit the room, Mrs. Colley began to make a recovery. She moaned and then muttered the word "hartshorn."

While the other men looked about the room for the remedy, Sir Maxim searched her reticule and pulled out a vial, which he held beneath her nose. Thus revived, she allowed the constable and Sir Maxim to help her to her feet.

She would not look at her son. Every time she attempted to do so, she blushed and inhaled deeply upon the hartshorn. She plopped down upon the dressing-table chair. For a moment she merely stared into space, then she said, "My necklace, where is my necklace?"

"What necklace, Mama?" the Squire asked innocently.

"Do not play games with me," she retorted, recovering her composure at last. "Jethro Gillingham, go to your room. I'll deal with you later, sir!"

"I'll go to my room, but I ain't stayin' there." As he raged toward the door, the Squire knocked the constable aside. "When a man can't have a little fun and gig in his own house without a swarm of busybodies barging in upon him, it's time to seek comfort elsewhere. I'm off to London where a man is given the respect that's his due. No more of these foreign wenches for me! The Colonel's given me the direction of a lady of the nobility. I tire of all these country bumpkins." He turned to exit.

Sir Maxim stood before the Squire, blocking his way. "You have caused the Contessa great embarrassment," he said, casting him a murderous glance. "You must apologize."

"Gentlemen pay off that sort of woman, they don't apologize to them." The Squire thrust out his chest. "Let me pass."

Maxim grinned slowly. "What would you know about being a gentleman?" He stared down the Squire for a moment. Then his gaze travelled to the discarded Apollo corset and he chuckled. "A man of your distension—er, distinction—shouldn't begin his struggles without his armour."

The Squire muttered a curse and squeezed out the door.

Glancing at Mrs. Colley, Maxim tried to feel pity for her, but failed. She wanted to believe the worst of everyone, and she'd tried to send Kate to gaol. He desired to have nothing further to do with the matron. "I must see to my sister," he said. "You, of course, will not wish to disturb her further by intruding upon her privacy tonight." He bowed slightly to Mrs. Colley. "Good night." Before he left her, he asked, "Have you troubled yourself to be concerned with what's happened to the Contessa?"

"What does it matter? She would have taken my necklace if he'd given it to her. I wash my hands of her."

As soon as the door closed behind him, Maxim's demeanor turned very grave. He would not leave Kate to manage on her own. She'd come close to being unmasked. That had been her second and final narrow escape from disaster. Getting her and Anthony safely away would require some ingenuity, but succeeding had become a point of honour. Not only had he promised Henry McClintock that the deed would be done, but some small, diabolic part of him longed to repay the Squire in kind. He would enjoy taking a hand in the retribution which Jethro Gillingham Colley deserved to have wreaked upon him.

Maxim scoffed at the notion that the source of his extreme ire with the Squire might be jealousy. He did admit to feeling peculiar when Kate played the part of the flirtatious courtesan with other men. Often he found it difficult to separate the act from the actress. Curiously, he had purposefully avoided the opportunity for a thorough self-examination since she had come to Ivel Manor. If he began any such mental exercise he found his thoughts becoming confused by interfering and audacious emotions.

Nonetheless, he couldn't avoid acknowledging that Kate sparked a reckless passion in him. Its intensity both alarmed and warmed him. However perplexing this state of being was, he knew one thing—he wanted to be with her.

And so, when he entered Lucy's bedchamber and saw Kate waiting for him, he felt that swift collision of emotions. He smiled fondly at her as if she and he were alone in the room. The intimacy of the look they exchanged was like an embrace.

After the moment of communion became noticeable, Anthony cleared his throat, breaking the spell between the two. "If I might claim your attention with a frivolous question, how are we to quietly withdraw from the manor, without drawing attention to ourselves?"

"We need a distraction," Sir Maxim stated, casting Kate a sidelong glance that indicated he certainly found her distracting.

Anthony emitted a gusty sigh, the force of which intimated his exasperation. "If you two continue ogling each other, we'll be here until the snows come."

"Just what sort of diversion did you have in mind, Max?" Lucy asked.

"I think the Squire, being the man he is, will provide us with just what we need," Maxim replied with a gleam in his eye.

As the first light of dawn crept over the landscape, a single shout of discovery sounded throughout Ivel Manor. "Aha!" cried Mrs. Colley, as she blocked the passage on the main stairs. "You thought you'd get away with it, did you? Jethro Gillingham Colley, hand over my necklace before I have the footmen turn your pockets out and search your travelling bags."

"This is an insult! My own mother suspects me of thievery! It's my opinion that you need to go to Bath and take the waters. All this nonsense about the Contessa and gypsies has deranged your mind." The Squire tried to step around his mother, but she moved from side to side with him.

"You'll not give my beautiful necklace to some demirep in Town. You may pay for your own favours." She grabbed for his coattails as he dashed by her. A rending of cloth followed as she held him fast.

"Look what you've done, Mother! You've ruined my best coat."

She plopped back on a step, holding on tenaciously. "What do clothes matter to you? You barely wear them anymore. Your activities of late don't require the niceties.''

"Mother!'' The Squire looked appalled.

"Don't assume the air of an innocent with me. You've revealed your true self. Now, hand over my jewels!''

Down the staircase came a line of servants laden with valises and trunks. As they lumbered by, they interrupted Mrs. Colley's harangue.

"Just how long do you plan to be in Town?'' she demanded of her son.

"Those aren't mine.''

They exchanged a puzzled look.

Then Lucy came down dressed in travelling attire, pulling on her gloves. "How kind of you to have risen so early to see us off, ma'am. I daresay my brother forgot to tell you we'd be leaving quite so soon.''

"But—but—'' stammered Mrs. Colley. "My dear child, you cannot leave me. Without your companionship I shall be utterly alone.''

"You'll have the Squire.'' Lucy smiled kindly, but would not yield.

"But Jethro has not paid his addresses to you.'' Mrs. Colley yanked at her son's coattails, ripping them further. "See what has come of your philandering? Now, do your duty! Ask her!''

"I pray he will not, ma'am,'' Sir Maxim said, as he descended the stairs with Kate at his side and Anthony trailing after. "As my sister's male protector, I must deem a man cut from Billingsgate cloth as being wholly ineligible. The Squire's misconduct with the Contessa is a clear example of how he treats women.''

He led his party out the front door towards his waiting carriage and team.

"What misconduct?" the Squire asked, as he and
his mother followed behind. "I never got the chance
to misbehave." He pulled out of his mother's grasp
and pointed to the Contessa. "There is your thief,
Mama! She took your necklace. Do not give your aid
to that stealing whore, Sir Maxim. Stand aside and let
us deal with the wanton as she deserves. If I had my
way she'd be the only woman aboard a ship full of
rutting convicts. They'd have her so often—"

Anthony had the Squire by the cravat before anyone else could react to the fellow's infamy. With a
quickness that caught the Squire off guard, he delivered a stunning blow to his jaw, effectively shutting his
mouth.

"We do not tolerate that sort of talk," Sir Maxim
stated coldly, "in the presence of our womenfolk. And
no one should speak of a lady in such a fashion." His
supercilious demeanour was as chill as the morning
air. "Well done," he murmured to Anthony as they
stepped over the Squire's inert form.

"Lady!" Mrs. Colley scoffed as she knelt beside her
son. "If the gossips are to be believed, she's sold her
goods so many times that they call her Secondhand
Sophia. I rue the day that I took her into my home.
She pretended to be a lady, but she's a harlot with no
heart. Just see what she has done to my son."

Sir Maxim gazed dispassionately at the uncon-
scious Squire. "He may consider himself lucky. Had
I laid hands on him he would likely never have re-

covered. See that he ceases to talk about the Contessa, else I'll return and finish what was started."

"You needn't take on so," Kate said soothingly to Maxim. "It appears that the Squire has got just what he deserves." Then she turned to Mrs. Colley. "But you should keep him at home, Ma'am, until he learns better conduct. Come along, Lucy, the carriage is waiting."

"Lucy, dearest!" Mrs. Colley wailed as she tried to crawl over her son towards the young lady. "Do not let her turn you against me. Please, whatever I've done, forgive me!"

"I daresay," Lucy remarked, "that I will come to forgive you after a time...after a very long time." She climbed into the chaise after Kate.

"It was a mistake," began Mrs. Colley.

"Yes, it was," Lucy said seriously. "One should never outstay one's welcome. Short visits are always the best."

"Goodbye, Mrs. Colley." Sir Maxim doffed his hat and stepped up into his carriage.

Coming out of his stupor, the Squire shook his head and gazed about dull-wittedly. "It is my opinion..." he began.

"Quite frankly," interposed Sir Maxim pleasantly, as he prepared to firmly close the door, "I don't give a damn about your opinion."

CHAPTER THIRTEEN

NOT LONG AFTER leaving Ivel Manor, Sir Maxim and his companions collectively expressed a renewed sense of freedom and an easing of tensions. A good deal of praise went to Lucy for her courage. And Anthony modestly accepted his sister's thanks for coming so quickly to her defense. Sir Maxim also received his share of compliments for his part in their hasty departure. All around they felt lighthearted.

"Luce," Sir Maxim said, "I think I must make you known to our travelling companions. This is—"

"Miss Katherina McClintock," Lucy interjected, "and her brother Anthony." She smiled confidently. "Not everyone thinks to treat me as a child, dear brother. Lieutenant McClintock—"

"It's Mr. McClintock," Anthony stated matter-of-factly, "now that I've sold out."

"*Mr.* McClintock," Lucy said with a friendly smile, "was kind enough to disclose his true identity to me during the May Day festivities. Besides, even under the most unusual circumstances, Katherina conducts herself as a lady, not a courtesan. But she hoodwinked everyone, did she not?"

"Not everyone," Kate murmured. "Sir Maxim knew me for an imposter from the very beginning."

"Did he?" Lucy gazed speculatively at her brother. "And he never gave you away or shared the secret. How gallant of you, Max."

"Gallantry, however, was not the impetus for my actions. It was my insatiable curiosity."

"Whatever the reason," Anthony said, "we are grateful for all of your assistance and discretion."

Kate seconded her brother's sentiments with a tentative smile, then glanced away from Maxim's searching gaze.

Long before the first change of horses the conversation in the carriage dwindled to silence. After staying up most of the night before, the party was soon overcome by a feeling of weariness and relief. Two of them drifted off to sleep. The other pair drifted with their thoughts.

The current of Kate's speculations carried her along at an alarming rate. She wondered if Maxim considered her indebted to him for the rescue. If so, what sort of payment would he require? Surely he would not use her unkindly. The thought that he might dishonour her chilled her to the bone.

Yet the recollection of his kisses warmed her thoroughly. Her need and desire to love Maxim was stronger than ever before. She felt exposed and vulnerable. If only he hadn't looked at her in just such a special way when he entered Lucy's room. If only her heart hadn't responded so entirely to the import of the moment. If only... if only.

If only, Maxim reasoned with himself, her soft green eyes were not so very fine. He might not have thought her such a striking beauty. If only her temperament were more caustic. He might have found her to be less of an agreeable companion. If only he didn't look forward to seeing her each day. He might have been able to walk away and go along...forgetting her after a time.

From his corner of the carriage, Maxim surreptitiously watched Kate. She stared out at the passing countryside, affording him the delightful aspect of her profile. Even though she no longer wore the veil, there was an intriguing air about her which he found vastly appealing.

As he studied her, he wondered what could be causing her brow to furrow and her lips to draw down despondently. He was overwhelmed with a desire to lift her burdens and shield her from any who would do her harm. Though a rather charitable fellow, especially where family and friends were concerned, he'd never felt so intensely protective before.

He began to quiz himself about her, and discovered to his dismay that although he knew her well, he knew very little about her. At the ripe age of five-and-twenty, she was considered a spinster, but had she ever wished to marry? What sort of life had she led before coming to Bedfordshire? She'd once mentioned something about being a lady's companion. Did she like labouring for others? And what of her family life? Had Henry McClintock given her much of a home to call her own?

He wondered what she would think of his home, Chiltern Hall. For some odd reason, which he did not yet want to examine, it was important to him that she like his home and those things about him that made him what he was.

A feeling of anticipation began to build within him as the day wore on and each stop and change of horses brought him closer to his estate. Though they made excellent time on the road, the sun was setting as the carriage left High Wycombe and rolled northward for a short stretch to Hughenden Valley.

Surrounded by a belt of trees, Chiltern Hall sat serenely on a ridge overlooking the valley. Built in the Baroque style, favouring the Italian with its fluted pilasters and magnificent windows, the house gave an impression of richness and variety. The central bays and uppermost storey created an illusion that the centre of the house projected further than it actually did. In the soft rays of the declining day, the brickwork and stone dressings took on a muted look which was inviting.

Maxim watched Kate closely to assess her response. She said nothing, but she gazed at the house at every opportunity that was given when the road leading up to it afforded a view. As the carriage halted in the gravel drive, she hardly waited to be helped down before she paused to examine the facade. A few shallow steps led up to the front door, which was held open by a polite butler.

As the party entered the house, Maxim felt a little anxious. Did she despise his taste in architecture? He glanced around at the Palladian entrance hall with its chequered black-and-white marble floor and screen of columns of blue-grey marble opening onto the staircase. Everything about the place pleased his eye.

Kate turned to him, appearing disconcerted. "It's very grand. I don't know why I never thought of you living in such a splendid house. Why do you ever leave here?" She gazed about in wonderment. "How comfortable, yet elegant, it is. 'Tis too fine to be left unattended by its master." Then, glancing upward at the painted ceiling, she smiled.

"The Roman influence," Maxim remarked, taking in stride the familiar sight of the bare-breasted maidens in the fresco.

Lucy joined them in their inspection of the ceiling. "The walls of the bathhouse are much more—" She flushed and darted a self-conscious look at Anthony. "They're more amply endowed . . . with colour, that is." She swallowed and grinned sheepishly. "Katherina, I must show it to you . . . when the gentlemen aren't with us. It's Maxim's newest addition to the estate—a fresh-water plunge bath housed in a delightful grotto."

Kate looked steadily at Maxim. Her eyes twinkled with amusement. "I should like very much to see it. Evidently Sir Maxim has a penchant for indulging in the whimsical. He must not be such a fusty old bookman as some have said."

"Oh, he loves books," Lucy blurted. "He treats them with more respect than he does many people."

"One must pay respect to those who've departed," Maxim observed, "and, for the most part, books are the works of those who've died."

Giving him a sidelong glance, Kate said, "I hope your library hasn't the appearance of a mausoleum."

"Alack and alas," he replied, matching her bantering tone, "but my improvements on the house as yet haven't reached the sublime. I've been waiting the advice of a certain lady. Though she is said to have been widowed at a very young age, she vows never to wear black again. A lady of obvious taste, wouldn't you agree, Miss McClintock? Now tell me," he said, taking her arm and leading her towards the stairs, "what is your opinion on an indoor bathing chamber, complete with an adjoining water closet?"

"Max!" Lucy exclaimed, clearly shocked by his free-and-easy manner with their guest.

Kate wrinkled her brow in consternation. "I regretfully admit my lack of knowledge concerning water closets. You must explain precisely what they are, Sir Maxim."

And thus began a week of tomfoolery the likes of which Chiltern Hall had never seen. It was as if Kate were trying to crowd a lifetime of living into just a few days. Acting as chaperons, Lucy and Anthony tried to keep apace with Kate and Maxim as they roamed the countryside on horseback and on foot, visited about the neighbourhood and stayed up late into the night playing cards or chess.

And all during this companionable time, Maxim refrained from quizzing Kate about her family and her past. Though she held him at a distance, she shared anecdotes with him and they played at besting each other with amazing stories of their youths.

When she told him of her father's scheme to recoup his lost fortune and settle his large debt, Maxim conceded that hers was the most fantastic tale. As she revealed all to him, he marvelled at her devotion to her family and her spirit of adventure. He hardly realized that she was at last telling him all that he'd wondered so long about. The quest for answers no longer seemed important. He simply enjoyed being with her.

Their constant association was having only one adverse effect on him. Every morning after rising and every night before retiring, he required a dousing in the cold waters of the plunge bath. He wasn't surprised when Anthony occasionally joined him for the ritual. There was a look of impatient torment in their eyes that each recognized in the other.

After a week of taking his cure, Maxim found that an additional dose was needed. On the day when Kate anticipated a reunion with the rest of her family, Maxim's amorous inclinations towards her were particularly keen. During luncheon he fought the impulse to nibble on the long column of her throat.

He tried to govern his thoughts, but lost the struggle when a hapless footman offered him a dish of roasted fowl—presented in the usual style with the meaty breast exposed to the view. He dared not look at Kate, to do so would have been insulting. To desire her was natural, but to compare her with fowl was unforgivable. He recognized that he was in a desperate state. Abruptly, he stood and excused himself.

The long walk he took only served to warm him further. A visit to the grotto seemed to be warranted. He hoped that the cold water would soothe his mind as well as his body.

The wooded area around the grotto was a perfect setting for the bathing house. The surrounding quiet was just what he needed to relax.

Impatient to begin, he chose not to use the upstairs dressing room, but instead intended to strip beside the pool. He began to remove his coat as he entered the bathing room. The sight that greeted his eyes stopped him, his coat hanging half off his shoulder. He stared for a long moment as an unsuspecting Kate swam slowly away from him.

Even though the bathing house was dimly lit, the waters were crystal clear. Maxim clapped a hand over his eyes as Kate turned about. She gasped.

"What the deuce are you doing in there, Kate?" Even his respect for her couldn't shake the notion that she was a dashed fine-looking woman.

"I—I was told you came to the bathhouse only in the morning and at night. You're not supposed to be here!"

He wondered if the quiver in her voice came from fright, cold, or— He smiled. Could she be amused by the situation?

A curious emotion began to overtake him. It was not arousal or desire, of that he was sure. It was as if some dark corner of his soul had been lighted by the noonday sun. He nearly dropped his hand from his eyes when he realized quite clearly that he loved Kate. *He loved her!*

"Kate, get out of that pool. I've things that I must say to you." He heard a movement in the water. "Kate?" He followed the sound of bare feet striking the marble floor. "Kate?" Water splashed against his cheek. He peeked between his fingers and saw her legs as she disappeared up the circular stairs leading to the dressing room.

"Don't peek, Maxim!" she shouted down.

"As soon as you're dressed," he called, shrugging his coat back on, "would you kindly meet me in the drawing room?"

"Very well, but, if you plan to scold me, I'll not stay."

"I've something different in mind," he replied.

He marched smartly up to the house and breezed by his butler, tossing back instructions that Miss McClintock was to be shown into the drawing room and then they were *not* to be disturbed. With the impatience of a bridegroom, he paced the floor. He stopped before a giltwood pier glass and checked his cravat. Catching himself in the act of primping, he laughed at his evident unsettled state.

Kate didn't keep him waiting long. But when she entered the drawing room he could see that she looked ill at ease. He smiled in a friendly manner, trying to indicate that nothing very awkward had occurred.

"You needn't leer at me," she said, with a decided edge in her voice. "It was a harmless mishap."

"Yes, it was. But I'm not leering at you."

She scowled at him. "You've a silly grin on your face. And must you stare at me in such a fashion?"

Clearly, he was handling the situation ineptly. He strolled to the fireplace, which was flanked by a pair of Corinthian pilasters. This setting might lend dignity to his endeavour.

"Kate, I wished to speak to you about a very particular matter. You must have noticed my regard for you, so this will not come as a surprise. Would you do me the great honour of becoming—"

"Don't you dare!" She flew at him and nearly slapped his cheek.

He caught her hands and held her firmly.

"Don't you dare propose marriage to me, Maxim—not after what passed in the bathhouse. It would be insulting."

"Insulting? The most splendid revelation—"

She raged in his arms. "Revelation! You did peek! If I were a man, I'd draw your cork!"

"Well, my dear, there's no doubt in my mind as to your gender. But that wasn't the sort of revelation I was speaking about." He stroked her hair gently and let his hand trail down to the side of her face. Looking into her eyes, he whispered earnestly, "I love you, Kate. I love you."

Tears filled her eyes. "Oh, Max." She leaned against him.

"And, being an honourable gentleman, I want to do the honourable thing. I want very much to marry you." He held her to him and kissed her ear and began to work downward to her throat.

She pulled back from him. "You needn't wed me just because you saw me naked. I would rather you asked me to become your mistress—not that I would—than think you must marry me because it's the honourable thing to do."

Holding her firmly by the arms, he stared at her for a time. "I distinctly remember you saying you were not a shrew. You lied. Katherina McClintock, I'll not tolerate this nonsense from a sensible lady like yourself. I am an honourable man. I am a man in love. I am *the* man who's going to marry you—willy-nilly, if it comes to that.''

Jerking away from him, she said, ''I am a dowerless girl. You are a man of property. You must marry well for the sake of your posterity.'' She backed away from him, twisting the silver ring on her little finger. ''Besides, you haven't shamed me. You needn't feel you must make a declaration.'' She hurried for the door.

''Dash it, Kate! Don't you dare go out that door. We haven't settled this. Kate! Come back here.'' He went after her and caught her in the hall. Without another word, he swept her into his arms and kissed her, then kissed her again.

Someone cleared his throat. ''It would appear that I've arrived just in time,'' Henry McClintock said calmly. ''Easy there, Polonius. One must expect this sort of thing in the springtime . . . in the country.''

Maxim raised his head, but retained his close hold of Kate. ''Thank God, you've come. Your daughter won't listen to me.''

Waving graciously for the couple to precede him, Henry indicated they should adjourn to the drawing room. He tossed the stunned Polonius his greatcoat and followed the couple in. He meandered over to the fireplace and, flipping aside his coattails, proceeded to give the room a thorough inspection.

''A very fine house, Sir Maxim,'' Henry commented. ''After spending nearly a sennight on the road, leading any who might try to follow on a false trail northward, I can appreciate the serenity of this beautiful country estate.'' Then, like a hawk swooping down on its prey, he asked sharply, "What the deuce do you mean by cuddling my daughter in front of the servants?"

"My intentions are honourable, sir," Maxim stated.

Both father and daughter made scoffing sounds.

Henry looked curiously at Kate. "There's something smokey here. And the sun will not set before I get to the truth of the matter. Now, make a clean breast of it, you two."

His reference to anatomy set the couple off into chuckles that built to laughter.

Wiping her eyes, Kate smiled tentatively at Maxim. "I forgive you for peeking. But that doesn't change," she added, as he began to move towards her, "my opposition to your proposal."

"Proposal?" Henry enquired in a suspicious tone. "What sort of proposal?"

"The honourable sort, sir," replied Maxim. "And, Kate, if you rail at me for being what I am . . . I shall know how to deal with you."

She bowed her head and sighed. "You are a gentleman of honour, and I have always been conscious of— and thankful for—your decorum and restraint under the most difficult of circumstances." She looked up and glanced about the room. "You have a very fine estate, but I will not share it with you as your wife. I am dowerless. I've been foolish beyond reason to allow my affection to become engaged. My father is not a wealthy man. And I've two brothers—one forced to sell out and the other without his schooling completed." She gazed into Maxim's eyes. "My deep affection for you prohibits me from burdening you with the millstone of an impoverished bride and her family.'' A tear slipped down her cheek. ''I will not marry you.''

Maxim stared at her, feeling the awesome weight of her refusal. He could see that she was quite determined to hold to her course. Willing to seek any source for advice—even that of a gamester-thespian—he turned to Henry, who rocked confidently on his heels.

''There's a way out of this quandry,'' Henry said, ''if you're both willing to take the gamble.''

CHAPTER FOURTEEN

THE INVITATIONS for the Wolverton Ball were delivered by special messenger to a select group of the ton. The exclusiveness of the guest list engendered great interest in the affair and the Town gossips made much of who was included and who was left off. Vying for an opportunity to attend by securing a place through another's invitation was the prime objective for many a lord and lady just days prior to the ball.

Since Sir Maxim was related to several of the prominent titled families he was assured that a large number of his guests would be coming. The close proximity of Chiltern Hall to Town—a mere three hours away— also guaranteed a handsome turnout for the affair.

And so, on the appointed day, a steady steam of arrivals disembarked at the front door of the Hall.

"Does anyone know if Lady Durston has arrived as yet?" Maxim asked in an aside to Anthony and Henry as they loitered in the upper gallery overlooking the entrance hall below.

"Patience," cautioned Henry. "She mustn't suspect anything. It is important that the bait be subtle—tempting enough to bring our bird to roost, but not so brassy as to frighten her away." He paused thoughtfully. "I hope Kate is resting. So much depends on her."

"You needn't worry, Papa," Anthony said, "she's got pluck and is as clever as her sire."

Henry frowned thoughtfully. "I don't doubt her abilities. But, though a most good-natured girl, when vexed she can be unpredictable. I should have told you about all the players in our little troupe, yet, as the master of a grand design, I needed to keep many things to myself." He sighed. "Sir Maxim, would you be so kind as to inform me when my old chum has arrived. I shall retire to my room now." He left them with the air of a man carrying a great load on his shoulders.

Anthony grinned at Maxim and said, "Above all else, he's an actor and must be excused for his theatrics." He shrugged and once again looked down at the entrance hall as the butler opened the door. "There's another group for you to greet, Sir Maxim. Do your duty."

Maxim did his duty all afternoon long, until his house was filled with members of the ton. Then, after a sumptuous dinner, he, along with Lucy, formally received their guests.

Standing at the foot of the stairs in the entrance hall, Lucy beamed proudly in evident enjoyment of the honour of being her brother's hostess. She leaned over to Maxim as an earl and his countess passed from them into the large drawing room. "It may sound quite mean-spirited of me," she whispered, "but I am glad Mama is stuck in the wilds of Yorkshire with Elizabeth and the new baby. This may be the last opportunity I have to act as your hostess." She smiled as another group of guests approached them and then said those polite things that were required of her.

During a subsequent lull, he squeezed her hand. "With a little luck, all will fall out as it should. When is Kate coming down?"

"Her father thought it best that they play least-in-sight until the ball gets under way." She graciously extended her hand to the next guests in line. "Lady Durston, how kind of you to come. And this must be your niece, the lovely young lady from Kent whom I've heard so much about." Turning to her brother, she said, "Maxim, you must thank your crony Mr. Hazeltine for bringing these ladies to our ball."

"Gustus, you rogue." Maxim took his friend's hand in a firm clasp. "You mustn't keep these ladies all to yourself. Lady Durston, I understand that you now and again enjoy a rousing game of piquet. Perhaps I might interest you in a hand or two tonight?"

Bedecked in enough jewels to make anyone stop and stare, Lady Durston fluttered her fingers, allowing the stones of her rings to catch the light. "Sir Maxim," she said in an innocent, childlike voice, "I can't im-agine who has been talking about me." She playfully poked Augustus in the side with her fan. "I tremble at the very thought of sitting across a gaming table from such a clever man as you. But the notion is so titillat-ing that I cannot deny you your request." She licked her lips, then fluttered her lashes at him from behind her opened fan.

Maxim noticed the *JGC* worked into the leaf design on the fan. "Have you been to Biggleswade of late, ma'am?"

"London keeps me amused," her ladyship replied. "I seldom venture into the Shires. But I do like the company of hearty country gentlemen. I made the recent acquaintance of one who thought himself lucky with the ladies and the cards."

"And was this buck of the first order successful with either?"

She held her fan against her breast, then closed it slowly to reveal a gold and ruby necklace. "I'll not tell you now. Perhaps later."

"After I've done my duties, then?" Maxim asked. "I know of a quiet room where we'll not be disturbed."

Lady Durston, a woman slightly past her prime, relayed coy messages to him with her fan. "Mr. Hazeltine," she said, not taking her eyes off Maxim, "you should have warned me about Sir Maxim and his way with the ladies. Until later." She gave Maxim a bashful look which turned quite warm with meaning.

Augustus herded the ladies before him. Over his shoulder, he cast Maxim an eloquent look, and in the process was almost felled by Colonel Buffard's wayward cane.

"My dear sir," Maxim said, aiding the spry old gentleman to a chair, "I see your gout is much improved, but your eye for the ladies remains the same."

The Colonel chuckled and jabbed Maxim with his cane. "I've got more than an eye for them. I must thank ye for the invite. There's ripe pickin's here to-night."

"It was at your crony's request that I sent the carriage for you. It's he you should thank." Maxim bowed slightly. "I trust you'll keep yourself innocently amused until you're needed."

The Colonel smiled guilelessly, but the moment a plump aristocratic matron strolled by, his cane came into play, lifting the lady's skirt for a peek of her ankle.

Maxim sighed and hoped for the best.

A short while later, the ball was being hailed as the event of the Season by those fortunate enough to be present. Everyone agreed that after weeks and weeks of jaunting about Town it was quite refreshing to get away to a place where they were sure there would be no encroaching persons of the lower order. The exclusivity of the guests was not diluted one whit, even when a party of four arrived late and joined the throng.

A whispered enquiry circled the drawing room as everyone wondered who the lady was Sir Maxim partnered for a second time. Was she a new, unknown heiress? The couple appeared to be on very good terms with each other.

Stepping to the lively tune of a Scotch reel, Kate tossed Maxim a saucy grin as she passed by him. When they clasped hands and twirled, her white muslin gown billowing out behind her, she remembered their ride together on the merry-go-round. She laughed to see him grimace in just the same way as he had when perched atop the wooden horse. Whirling about apparently wasn't his favourite pastime.

"Are you feeling quite the thing?" she asked as the dance concluded.

He closed his eyes tight. "Quite frankly, I hardly know if I'm on my head or my heels. Is my unsettled state due to the dance or your father's circumvolving plan for retrieving his fortune? If only the room would stop spinning. This is hardly the night I want to be without my senses." Gradually he opened his eyes. "Have you seen Lady Durston of late?"

After glancing about the room, she shook her head and said, "Papa says that Lady Durston will either be tossing a pair of the ivories or tossing up her skirts for some—oh, dear." She flushed slightly. "I shouldn't have said such things to you." She hid her head in the curve of his shoulder.

"Kate, if you're going to become missish now, I'll tell you plain, dear girl, it's too late." With a coaxing lift of his finger he helped her to look up at him. "I know you for the outspoken and stubborn woman that you are, and I quite like you, all the same. It baffles me why your brothers continue to think of you as amiable," he remarked in a teasing tone.

She gasped and ducked her face into his shoulder again.

"Kate? What the deuce is ailing you?"

"The Colonel," she whispered, peeking around his arm to confirm what she'd seen. "Why is he here, Maxim?"

He glanced back and cocked his head, acknowledging the gentleman. The Colonel saluted in return.

"You still don't know?" enquired Maxim. "I must admit nor did I until your father insisted the old fellow be among the invited. It was then he disclosed the history of their acquaintance and the wisdom of his casting."

Kate cautiously peered at the Colonel, who winked at her.

Maxim claimed her attention by saying, "He may be a novice thespian, but the Colonel is a master swordsman. He was cast as the frisky old roué, a part much to his character."

"You needn't tell me about the Colonel's character," she retorted with a catch of amusement. "Do recall I've been the subject of his admiration."

He winced. "I need no reminder. Your father wanted you to have an extra protector lurking in the background." He looked at her and they chuckled together. "I doubt he was thinking of him as that sort of protector. But for the plot to succeed he deemed it advisable not to acquaint all the players with each other."

"Papa did say he had a trick or two up his sleeve, but his chicanery goes beyond all bounds." She fanned herself briskly. "I daresay the Colonel is here for the last act of our little performance."

He proffered his arm to her. "Then let the act begin. Shall we find Gustus and our pigeon?" Smiling and nodding to his guests as he and Kate made their way to the door, he murmured, "I hope—though it's doubtlessly foolish to do so—that your father has behaved himself."

"He is probably about somewhere trying to convince a wealthy lord of the wisdom of investing in a partnership in a theatre. Polonius is to keep watch over him." As they climbed the main staircase, she felt a qualm and sense of foreboding. "Maxim, should we fail tonight, please do not press me further." She paused as the significance of her words threatened to overcome her resolve. "Your family connections are far superior to mine; your circumstances are much more exalted than mine. I could not ask you to enter into such a misalliance."

He was silent until they reached the upper gallery. After making sure they were not observed, he kissed her tenderly, then, holding her hands, he said earnestly, "You are the only woman I wish to marry. What care I if you are dowerless?"

She became keenly aware of the ring on her little finger hidden beneath her glove. "You *ought* to care, for your children's sake."

"Not everything I possess is entailed. In my own right, I'm quite comfortably situated. Let me take care of you, Kate."

"Marriage scarcely signifies when a woman must be kept by a man. I've never liked the idea of being a possession which had to be bought." Perhaps it was foolish pride, but she would not go to him as a beggar. And though her father had made a slight recovery, he still owed a debt of fifteen thousand guineas to Lady Durston. How could she demand he give her a marriage portion when he might be required to go to debtors' prison? She didn't want the love she and Maxim shared burdened by the weight of her family's troubles.

"I don't want to own you," he said, "but merely love you and share my life with you."

Bravely, she smiled at him. "We'd best put the matter aside for a time. With luck..."

"Then...for luck," he murmured, cupping her face in his hands. He kissed her as if he wanted her to take all his strength and courage.

And she hungrily clung to him, feeling this might be the last time he held her. As he drew away, she gazed up at him, her green eyes bright with a hint of tears. "'Men at some time are masters of their fates.' Tonight is our time. Come, Maxim, let us challenge chance and rise forth as the victors," she said, her tone fired with determination.

He smiled at her, his dimples coming into play. "I almost feel sorry for Lady Durston. She will have a formidable foe."

They parted with a strong sense of purpose. Following a carefully conceived plan, Maxim left to execute his important part of it, drawing in the pigeon, while Kate went off to seek out Augustus.

Maxim discovered Lady Durston as she came out of an antechamber. She paused to straighten the bodice of her gown and smooth the wrinkles from her skirt. The heated flush on her cheeks hinted at unusual exertions on her part.

"Milady, have you been dancing?" he asked, in a dubious tone.

In a titillating fashion, she fingered the gold and ruby necklace which lay upon her breast. "Dancing? Yes, you may say I've taken a turn or two on the floor." She fluttered her lashes and assumed an innocent mien. Taking his arm, she managed to jiggle so that the gems at her exposed bosom flashed in the light. "Didn't you promise me a game ... of piquet?"

"I've come to learn if you are still desirous of a hand or two. But perhaps you should be returning to your niece."

"The dear girl is being chaperoned by her god-mama. We needn't concern ourselves with her." She pressed against him. "Shall we find a quiet room?" When he turned to open the door she'd just exited, she held him back from entering. "Not in there. I believe it is occupied." She led him down the corridor. "In such a large house there must be a special place where we'll not be bothered by intruders."

"My library will serve."

Known as a hidden library, the room was panelled in oak, and each panel between the pilasters swung open at the touch of a stud to reveal a filled book-case. The classical style of the chamber hardly seemed conducive to seduction. Maxim felt as if he insulted the consequence of this revered place of study by al-lowing Lady Durston to enter.

He grimaced when she reclined upon the sofa on which he'd spent many happy hours stretched out, reading and thinking. The notion of gaining carnal knowledge of this aging wanton in that same place sickened him. Strolling to a pair of upholstered chairs with a gaming table placed between them, he indi-cated that she should join him.

"You were in earnest about the game?" she asked in surprise.

He grinned at her with half-closed eyes. "I've dis-covered that a bit of play beforehand adds a certain liveliness to the final moment of surrender.'' She was in the seat opposite him before he could conquer his self-disgust for having made such a statement.

The pretense of innocence Lady Durston liked to project fell away to be replaced by the obvious lures of a cheap harlot. She used her tongue and fingers to convey messages that a blind man could have read.

Though impervious to her overblown charms and enticements, Maxim repeatedly lost and played along as if he could not concentrate on the cards in his hands.

Clearly, her confidence and boldness grew with each game she won. Soon her fever for gaming took hold. While attacking his leg with her unshod foot, she bet with reckless abandonment.

She leaned forward to scoop up the notes he'd written—her winnings. Her breasts appeared in danger of spilling out of her décolletage.

Praying for intervention, he looked away to the clock. ''How late it is becoming. I shall have to return to my guests soon.''

Breathing heavily, apparently more stimulated than was warranted, Lady Durston sank back in her chair and fingered the blood-red stones of her necklace. ''I'll not let you go until I've collected what you owe me. Shall we play for just a while longer—making the wager more interesting?'' She licked her lips. ''I'll bet my garters and stockings—''

''Maxim!'' Augustus advanced into the room along with Kate. ''I've been looking for you everywhere,'' he said significantly. ''What is the meaning of hiding here in your fusty bookroom when you've guests asking after you? Ah, Lady Durston, how fortuitous. I've a lady here who's been wanting to meet you. Let me make you known to Miss—'' He mumbled the last name, then coughed. "Must have some wine."

While Augustus coughed, Maxim offered to fetch them all some refreshment. He excused himself, indicating to Lady Durston by a look that nothing would keep him long from her side.

"Lady Durston," Kate began, "how pleased I am to meet you." She glanced down at the table. "Have we interrupted your game? Do forgive us. Nothing is so vexing as being disturbed in the middle of play."

Lady Durston glared at her, as if wanting to extract a payment for her intrusion.

"Well, my dear," Augustus said rather thoughtfully, "you might take Sir Maxim's place until he returns. Her ladyship is a keen player, who would no doubt oblige you."

Gathering the cards, Lady Durston asked, "Do you care for piquet, young woman? I am very fond of it." With a smug expression, she added, "But the stakes must be high. I will not play for paltry sums." At Kate's nod of consent, she dealt the required number of cards.

Kate lost the first game and the next. Vouched for by Augustus, she signed over five thousand of her father's guineas. She tried not to think of the game in terms of guineas lost. Above all else, she needed to concentrate on piquing Lady Durston's interest. If her ladyship lost too soon, she would be discouraged from continuing. If she won too easily, she would walk away in disgust.

"I must tell you, Lady Durston, that my Papa would be thoroughly irritated," Kate remarked ingenuously, "if he learned that I was disposing of his fortune so readily—even this meagre portion of it. He thinks that every penny must be saved until it is a pound. I believe that most men of great wealth are of the same mind."

"You are a woman of means, then?" Lady Durston appeared interested.

Kate modestly lowered her lashes. "It would be ill-mannered of me to boast."

"Shall we raise the stakes?" her ladyship asked politely, though the fire in her eyes gave away her obsession to win all her opponent owned.

With ladylike hesitation, Kate agreed.

Before play could resume, Maxim came in with a tray of glasses and a pair of bottles. "Forgive my interruption," he said, glancing at the notes Lady Durston held. "Have you occupied yourselves while I was gone?"

Her ladyship eyed him sulkily. "I was amusing myself until your return, but now that the stakes are quite high I cannot break away. It has become a challenge."

Maxim offered the ladies some ratafia, then handed his crony a full goblet of Madeira.

Augustus first looked at the brimming glass with a perplexed expression. Then, with dawning comprehension, he cleared his throat loudly and sipped. His eyes conveyed a question to Maxim, who inclined his head towards the door.

A group of distinguished guests entered the library and Colonel Buffard, as their self-appointed spokesman, demanded to know what was detaining their host.

"We have a contest of sorts," Maxim explained, "between these two ladies. Her ladyship has just raised the stakes."

To the gentlemen, Augustus muttered, "It's cutthroat piquet." An excited murmur passed among those who gathered around the gaming table to watch.

Lady Durston set her wine aside and dealt the cards. For a time she controlled the game, then, bit by bit, Kate's skill and intuitive powers turned the odds in her favour. But just as she was about to retrieve all she'd lost, Lady Durston rallied and began winning again.

Augustus and Maxim exchanged a worried look. Leaning on the back of Lady Durston's chair, Maxim watched the play closely, then he signalled his friend, who nodded his understanding and motioned for Maxim to distract her ladyship.

Under the pretense of offering Kate more wine, Augustus whispered, "She's been marking the figured cards with one of her rings."

"I know, but I dare not call her on it. We must continue gaming." Kate thoughtfully glanced at the diamond pin nestled in the folds of his cravat. "Slip me your pin and I'll endeavour to nullify that female sharp's cheating ways."

Augustus palmed his pin and passed it to her. "I hope you know what you're doing. There'll be the devil to pay if this fails."

She smiled confidently. When play resumed, she surreptitiously marked some of the lower cards in a manner that indicated they were of higher value. It wasn't until the following hand that she noticed the perplexed expression on Lady Durston's face as she ran her fingers over the little marks.

With narrowed eyes, her ladyship looked across at Kate and pursed her lips in dissatisfaction.

Kate let her opponent catch a glimpse of the pin, then she cast her ladyship a challenging look, which was answered with a brief nod of assent. The woman would play fair. It was time for a new deck of cards, but calling for one without casting suspicion on her ladyship presented a problem. By a series of eloquent glances, Kate conveyed to Maxim the gist of her predicament.

Leaning over her ladyship's shoulder, Maxim offered her more wine and began to pour. He feigned a look of admiration as he diverted his gaze from the glass to her obvious charms.

She responded with a sultry smile, then, with eyes widening, she squealed and grabbed for her notes of IOU from Kate. "The wine, Sir Maxim! You're spilling it all over."

"How clumsy of me, ma'am. I've ruined the cards." He rang for a footman and ordered a new deck.

Thus neatly scotched in her efforts to cheat, Lady Durston began to play without the use of any devices. Her fevered desire to win at all costs seemed to cloud her judgement, and as she steadily began to lose, she wagered more heavily.

Word of the game somehow spread and soon quite an audience collected to watch. Many of the gentlemen whispered among themselves that the play was as deep as any to be found at the clubs. They marvelled that ladies of Quality could play with such daring and dash.

Apparently keeping close track of her growing losses, Lady Durston stared at the cards dealt her. She would not touch them. Instead she sat back and thoughtfully fanned herself. "I grow weary. Shall we continue this tomorrow when we are not so distracted by the others?"

Before Kate could answer, Augustus enquired in a haughty tone, "Haven't you the bottom to stay the course, ma'am? Is it courage or funds you lack?"

The room abruptly grew very quiet. With several leaders of the ton looking on, a lady gamester dare not admit she was shy of the funds or the mettle to support further play. It was permissible to withdraw when winning, but to retreat a loser was thought an act of cowardice.

Kate placed her cards on the table. Glancing at the slips of paper Lady Durston had signed, she calculated her winnings. As nearly as she could tell by her quick reckoning, the amount was slightly more than her father had lost.

She picked up her cards. "There is something in your possession that I want very much."

"My necklace? Please—it was bestowed as a token of deep affection. I could not part with it." Lady Durston glanced about nervously.

"At the first of the year," Kate said, "the deed of a theatrical property came into your hands. Also, you hold the note of one Henry McClintock. These I desire." Kate took a handful of her ladyship's vowels and placed them in the middle of the table. "The value of your notes is at least that of the property and the one IOU. However, there is still the question of a fortune to restore. Do you care to play, milady?"

With trembling hands, her ladyship took up her cards and spread them in a fan. She licked her lips and looked to Kate to start.

Kate discarded one card, indicating her confidence in the strength of her cards, which consisted mostly of aces, kings, queens, and knaves with a good sequence of hearts. She drew a nine of hearts, increasing the run of her suit.

Throwing down five cards, Lady Durston made her discard and drew her cards one at a time. She bit her lip.

After completing the ritual of calling point, sequence and *quatorze*, Kate's score numbered over thirty, leaving her ladyship with nothing.

Lady Durston gasped, along with the others watching. The quick rise and fall of her necklace on her breast indicated her agitation. "Very well," her ladyship whispered, her voice raw with desperation, "you have a *repique*, but do not think you can beat me thoroughly. Play on!"

They did play on, and Kate took nearly every trick.

"You must allow me another chance to recoup my winnings." The older woman looked aged and wild-eyed. "Deal! We must play another hand."

Kate ignored the hysterical woman and looked beyond the faces of those urging her to continue. In the back of the crowd, shaded from the revealing light, stood her brothers and her father. She looked at him for guidance, but received no indication as to what she should do.

Her gaze travelled from her father to Maxim, who regarded her quietly. Finally she turned her attention to her ladyship.

After clutching the ruby and gold necklace, Lady Durston unclasped it and flung it on the table. "There's my stake. I won it from a loutish squire. It is quite valuable. Does it tempt you?" She appeared reckless and frantic.

Kate shook her head slowly.

"No?" Her ladyship's voice quavered, as if on the verge of breaking into sobs. "Then I will also stake my carriage and my team. Surely now you will agree to play on!"

CHAPTER FIFTEEN

DISPASSIONATELY, Kate continued to watch her opponent. Her silent regard seemed to unnerve the woman.

"Still not enough?" Lady Durston tore the rings from her fingers and slammed each one down, saying, "Here! Here! Take this one, too. Take them all, but you must play me. You must! I'll not be bested by a nobody. How dare you act so condescending, so—so virtuous! Who *are* you, anyway?"

"I'll say my name quite clearly so you'll never forget it." Kate leaned forward and stared her ladyship in the eye. "I am Katherina McClintock, daughter of Henry McClintock."

Lady Durston's eyes narrowed to slits and her nostrils pinched together in a tight expression of great anger. She glanced from the pile of notes resting on the table before Kate to the full wineglass at her side. With a purposeful wave of her fan, her ladyship tipped the glass.

Before one drop of wine spilled, Colonel Buffard flourished his cane in a series of quick parrying taps on either side of the glass. He steadied it with side-to-side touches of his walking stick at the shoulder of the bowl.

A collective sigh escaped the viewers at this handy bit of swordplay. "Well done, sir!" Augustus clapped the Colonel on the back.

Completely vanquished, her ladyship sank back against the chair, her mouth gaping open in astonishment. She clutched her hands to her chest and sank lower, as if trying to hide. "I meant no harm. It was all a game. I must always win. I must."

"Tonight you lose. I'll not play on," Kate said, gathering together her ladyship's vowels. "There is no sport in gaming with such sorry creatures as you, Lady Durston."

"But I took everything of your father's. I left him with nothing." The older woman scooped up her jewels and held them high. "You must want all that is mine."

Henry stepped forward and assisted her ladyship to her feet. "You have nothing that my daughter would value, ma'am. And if you thought you'd left me with nothing, you were mistaken. I had my luck, my friends, my children...and a grand design for the McClintock destiny. You have your jewels, your house, your carriage and much more, but you are poor. A moral bankrupt...and mean of spirit." He shook his head sadly. "A pitiful creature."

Backing away, she glanced about at the onlookers. "You are my friends. Wait! Don't turn your backs on me! Will no one come to my aid?" She cast herself in Maxim's arms. "Help me. Please!"

Together with the aid of Augustus and the Colonel, Maxim ushered Lady Durston from the library.

An awkward pause hung in the air. Henry, ever the showman, claimed centre stage. "And thus concludes a sample of the new play entitled *A Lady's Lament: or Just Deserts*. We hope you enjoyed our little offering. Pray excuse Lady Durston for the remainder of the evening, as her role was most strenuous and she must rest." He bowed when a few of the bystanders clapped and then he motioned towards the door.

Those who'd watched the spectacle quietly filed out, looking puzzled, as if they couldn't quite distinguish fancy from fact. Some even complimented Henry on the unusual production and asked when their friends might view it, too. In his typical fashion, Henry sidestepped the enquiries and airily said that there was much to do before the play could go before the public. Graciously, he saw the last guest out.

The McClintocks lingered in the library. They were all silent for a time.

Gazing at her father in a quizzical manner, Kate tried to divine the elusive man. "*A Lady's Lament*?" she enquired sceptically.

"An appropriate title—given the circumstances," Henry said phlegmatically. With one hand on his hip and the other raised to his brow, he paused thoughtfully. "It was inspiration, actually—coming from I know not where. Perhaps the Bard was trying to tell me something. I've had this notion—almost like an inexplicable prompting—that I should pick up the pen and write. *A Lady's Lament: or Just Deserts* shall be my first work."

"I know just the actress to play Lady Durston," Polonius said excitedly. Father and son shared a look of discovery. "Siddons!" they said together.

Henry joyously embraced his younger son, then held him at arm's length. "I had hoped that one of my children would show an inclination to follow after their sire. As you showed promise, I tried not to influence you unduly. But our minds are now so akin that I do you a disservice in keeping you from me. If you desire, Polonius, you may act as my assistant and manage the theatre on my behalf—that is, as soon as I recover my real property from Lady Durston." He cast his beaming smile upon Anthony and Kate. "Your futures are repaired, children. I shall engage a man of business to see that they remain so. I'll send him round, first thing, to collect what her ladyship owes me."

"But it is Kate who holds her notes," Anthony remarked gently.

Kate handed her father the IOUs—a hefty handful of them. "It was your stake I used, Papa, and I only acted on your behalf. I am sure these were meant for you no matter who played for you."

Hugging her to him, Henry wiped his eye. "Since I now have the ready, I daresay you'll be wanting to wed. A dowry of four thousand pounds should do nicely."

She drew back from him. "Thank you, Papa. But what of Tony? His future is most unsettled."

Anthony chuckled lightheartedly. "Tonight Sir Maxim did me a great service. He introduced me to the Earl of Liverpool. After conversing with him at length, I was offered a post. I shall have the honour of assisting the Secretary of War, no less. His lordship is a man of great influence, and I hope to learn much from him. My future may not be secure, as yet, but it has bright possibilities." He looked at Kate pointedly. "Well, what are you waiting for? We don't get many chances for happiness. You'd best go claim yours."

She lifted her skirts and hurried to the door. Halfway there she halted and turned back. "Papa, can you promise to give up wagering? I only ask as I've no desire to play the Contessa again."

Henry frowned. "I promise I shall be quite busily engaged in writing the very best play since Shakespeare. Should I fail, I'll merely borrow from the Bard. But I assure you, my dear, I would not want my family to become a burden upon your husband. This ordeal has drained me. I daresay I'll not touch the cards for at least a fortnight." Unconsciously, he thumbed a pack of cards.

With a resigned sigh, she grinned at her brothers, who shooed her from the room. She hurried down the corridor to the entrance hall, then descended the staircase. Before she could find Maxim she stumbled upon Augustus in the drawing room, where he was watching the dancers.

"May I congratulate you?" he asked with exuberant good spirits.

For a moment Kate was taken aback. Had Maxim said something to his crony to indicate an approaching nuptial celebration? "I beg your pardon?"

"That was a dashed fine display of gaming. Thought for a while we might not get out of the basket. But all's well that ends well, hey?" Augustus smoothed a wrinkle from his sleeve. "Lady Durston was a little reluctant to leave, but she stopped being a loggerhead when she realized Maxim wasn't about to make her his inamorata. She took herself off to High Wycombe in high dudgeon."

"I thought I might enjoy heaping revenge upon Lady Durston," Kate remarked. "But I merely feel sorry for the miserable woman. Watching her reveal the dark parts of her soul was like observing her disrobe before all the company."

"Well," he said ponderously after a moment of consideration, "she would have looked a dashed sight better if she'd gone about in her shift, rather than that awful gown she was almost wearing."

She tried not to laugh with him, for it was rather cruel to make light of the poor woman, but he was too likeable to resist.

"I've the strangest feeling," he said, "that we've met before, but I can't place where." He worried over the matter until a pretty girl passed before his view. Excusing himself, he almost caught up to her at the door, but was waylaid by a cane to the shin.

"What do you say if we play this one as a team?" Colonel Buffard asked in a breathy voice. "I fancy her mother."

Left alone to look about the room, Kate felt an awareness prior to hearing the voice behind her.

"'Come live with me, and be my love, and we will some new pleasures prove—'" Maxim smiled at her as she turned round.

Her old shyness overtook her at that moment and she glanced down. But before she was completely vanquished by her own timidity, the new flame that burned within her warmed her blood and gave her a sense of the great power of love. She returned his look fully.

"That's not Shakespeare," she replied with a twinkle.

"No, it's not. The time has come to broaden your interests." Maxim took Kate's hand in his.

Without further ado, he led Kate out to the garden, saying he'd had his best luck with her out of doors. Hardly had they wandered from the lights of the house before he dropped his decorous manner and swept her into his arms.

Of all the kisses they'd exchanged, this was the sweetest, for it was the first without obstacles to impair it or guilt to taint it. It was so delightful that he repeated it over and over again until they were weak, but quite warm from their loving.

"Katherina McClintock, would you honour me by consenting to be my wife? I love you, Kate. I love you more each day, and, at the alarming rate of growth of my sentiments, I'll have you ravished in a fortnight if you say no. Please say you will wed me, and wed me soon." He held her hands tightly in his. "You had better find more of those little rings like the one on your finger, my dear. Just the one will not suffice for the family we'll be having."

She smiled slowly. "I recommend that you have the banns read on Sunday next. I would not want my betrothed behaving precipitously." She kissed him lightly on the chin. "You'll have to suffer the rigours of the plunge bath for a few more weeks."

"Is that a yes?"

"Yes, of course, Maxim, I'll marry you. Was there ever any question that I wouldn't do so?"

His lips captured her teasing ones and taunted them in a fashion that left her compliant. His hands moved slowly down her back and came to rest at her hips.

"How fortunate the Season hasn't ended," he murmured in her ear. "Otherwise we might have some of these guests under foot for far too long. And I'm looking forward to a very private honeymoon...spent in the grotto," he caressed her lower back and added, "looking for your moles."

She chuckled softly. "That sounds very wicked. But I pray this passion is of a lasting sort," she said, leaning against him, "since with a family such as mine there is bound to be an uncertain future. I'll try to find some way to thank you for all your help...especially the kindness you did for Tony."

"He's a good fellow. Just the type of man Lucy needs, but they'll have to find their own happiness. For quite a while, he'll not be in a position to seek a wife, but given time he'll come into his own. We each must make the best of what life gives us." He demonstrated his point by kissing her quite thoroughly. "For, after all," he murmured with a whimsical smile, "life is a merry go-around."

Harlequin Regency Romance™

COMING NEXT MONTH

#31 A COUNTRY CHIT by Emily Dalton
"Kitty" Whitchurch could never resist using her high-spirits and resourceful wit to outmanoeuver a man. So when Lord Nathan Hatherleigh expressed his doubts about her ability to catch a husband before the end of summer, Kitty took up the challenge with alacrity. But little could she have known that Lord Hatherleigh was secretly at work undoing her efforts for reasons of his very own.

#32 THE LEMON CAKE by Judith Stafford
Who ever heard of firing off four young ladies in one Season? Under the careful supervision of their aging but loveable aunt, Miss Abby Milhouse and her three sisters became the toast of town. Each of them in turn received the attentions of an eligible parti, until their aunt, Lady Jeffrey, revealed the secret of their success. An old recipe, a little magic and voilà, the lemon cake!

Coming in July
From America's favorite author

JANET DAILEY

Fiesta San Antonio
Out of print since 1978!

The heavy gold band on her finger proved it was actually true. Natalie was now Mrs. Colter Langton! She had married him because her finances and physical resources for looking after her six-year-old nephew, Ricky, were rapidly running out, and she was on the point of exhaustion. He had married her because he needed a housekeeper and somebody to look after his young daughter, Missy. In return for the solution to her problems, she had a bargain to keep.

It wouldn't be easy. Colter could be so hard and unfeeling. "I don't particularly like myself," he warned her. "It's just as well you know now the kind of man I am. That way you won't expect much from our marriage."

If Natalie had secretly hoped that something would grow between them— the dream faded with his words. Was he capable of love?

Don't miss any of Harlequin's three-book collection of Janet Dailey's novels each with a Texan flavor. Look for *FOR BITTER OR WORSE* coming in September, and if you missed *NO QUARTER ASKED* . . .